TWO FOR THE DEVIL

ALLEN HOFFMAN

SmallWorlds

ABBEVILLE PRESS
PUBLISHERS
NEW YORK
LONDON
PARIS

JACKET FRONT:
"Adolf Hitler": Archive Photos; "Joseph Stalin": Popperfoto/Archive Photos.

EDITOR: SALLY ARTESEROS
DESIGNER: CELIA FULLER
PRODUCTION EDITOR: MEREDITH WOLF SCHIZER
PRODUCTION DIRECTOR: HOPE KOTURO

FIRST EDITION
2 4 6 8 10 9 7 5 3 1

LIBRARY OF CONGRESS CATALOGING-IN-PUBLICATION DATA
HOFFMAN, ALLEN.
TWO FOR THE DEVIL / ALLEN HOFFMAN.
P. CM. — (SMALL WORLDS : [3])
ISBN 0-7892-0397-9
1. JEWS—RUSSIA—FICTION. I. TITLE. II. SERIES: HOFFMAN, ALLEN.
SMALL WORLDS : 3.
PS3558.034474T96   1998
813'.54—DC21   98-16026

For Bob Abrams,
Publisher and Friend

Is my strength the strength of stones?
or is my flesh of brass?

—Job 6:12

THE LETTER

FOR YEARS THE REBBETZIN, SHAYNA BASYA, DUTIFULLY placed Postum and Aunt Jemima pancakes before the rebbe in the morning, and Yaakov Moshe Finebaum dutifully consumed them. After breakfast, the rebbetzin placed pen and paper on the rebbe's desk; but even though he spent long hours alone in his study, the rebbe never touched them. When she encouraged him to write to their daughter, Rachel Leah, in Russia, he would nod agreeably and explain, "When the time is right."

There were moments when the rebbetzin thought the time might be right. In 1923, after Warren Harding died and Silent Cal Coolidge entered the White House, the rebbetzin noticed that the pen and paper had been used. But one morning, the rebbe pointed with disgust at a campaign picture in the St. Louis newspaper of Calvin Coolidge posing in an Indian warbonnet. In the background, his chauffeur and limousine waited to whisk him away. "An impostor, a fake," the rebbe declared angrily and stalked into his study. The next morning, Shayna Basya again found the writing materials untouched.

They remained that way until 1927, when Charles A. Lindbergh made his historic solo flight across the Atlantic. "The Spirit of St. Louis," the rebbe mused conspiratorily, savoring the name of the heroic aviator's craft. "Our son-in-law, Hershel Shwartzman, could fly it back here for him," he suggested, picking up the pen. The rebbetzin didn't respond. As far as she knew, Grisha, their son-in-law, couldn't pilot a plane. Even if he could, Lindbergh had flown solo; there wasn't any room in the "Spirit of St. Louis" for Rachel Leah. It made no difference, however, for the rebbe suddenly ceased writing when the newspaper worshipfully referred to Lindbergh as the "Lone Eagle." "A *trayf* bird, grasping impurity," he pronounced, sadly shaking his head. Despairing of his ever writing to their daughter, Shayna Basya stopped providing him with pen and paper.

In 1936, Reb Zelig, the rebbe's sexton, fell ill and died. On a steamy summer day, they buried him, and upon returning from the cemetery, the rebbetzin opened the icebox for a cool drink.

"Would you like something?"

"Yes," he answered, sweat covering his smooth forehead in an unbroken watery film, as if he had just surfaced from a deep pool.

"What?" she asked.

"A pen and paper," he demanded.

"Whatever for?" she asked.

"If I don't write now, the letter won't arrive before Rosh Hashanah," he explained matter-of-factly.

The rebbetzin followed him into the study and presented him with pen and paper. "Thank you," he said, and began writing at once.

Fifteen minutes later, she was sipping a cool glass of water at the kitchen table when the rebbe returned with the letter.

"That was quick," she commented.

"Sixteen years, and you call it 'quick,'" the rebbe said, slightly bemused.

"Would you like a drink?" she asked.

"A beer, please."

She looked up in surprise. The rebbe had never shown any taste for the beverage.

"Yes, Prohibition is over," he stated.

She placed the cool bottle on the table; at once a fine mist shrouded its dark surface. She pushed the letter away so it wouldn't get wet.

"Thank you," he said, but she didn't answer.

She was staring down at the envelope addressed to her son-in-law. Prohibition had ended in St. Louis. The rebbetzin wondered how her daughter and son-in-law were welcoming Rosh Hashanah, the New Year, in Moscow in 1936.

I
ROYAL GARMENTS

If a king's porphyra, royal purple garment, appears as merchandise in the market square, woe unto the seller and woe unto the buyer. Thus Israel is the royal purple garment in whom the Holy One is glorified for it is written "Israel in whom I (God) am glorified . . ." (Isaiah 49:3) and, consequently, if Israel becomes common merchandise, it is woe unto the seller and woe unto the buyer.

—Midrash Esther Rabba

MOSCOW
1936

ROSH HASHANAH
(THE NEW YEAR)

It is taught in the name of Rabbi Eliezer that the Sixth Day of Creation fell on Rosh Hashanah, the New Year. On that day Adam was created from the dust, was placed in the Garden, was commanded not to eat of the Tree, sinned, in the eleventh hour he was judged, and in the twelfth hour he was pardoned. The Holy One Blessed Be He said to Adam: Just as you stood before Me in judgment on this very day, Rosh Hashanah, and you were pardoned, thus in the future your sons will stand before Me in judgment on Rosh Hashanah and they, too, will be pardoned.

—Vayikra Rabba

Rabbi Yossi Bar Kazarta taught: The Holy One Blessed Be He said to them, since you entered in judgment before Me on Rosh Hashanah and went forth in peace, I consider you as if you are a new creation.

—Jerusalem Talmud, Tractate Rosh Hashanah

PATRIARCHS AND PROGENY

NEITHER YAAKOV MOSHE FINEBAUM, THE KRIMSKER Rebbe, nor Karl Marx, the social philosopher, ever visited Moscow. Both, however, engendered offspring who resided in the traditional capital of Russia.

Karl Marx, the father of scientific socialism, based his materialistic determinism on the critical dialectic. The critical dialectic taught that the interaction of antagonistic, dynamic forces leads to change, and these new developments in turn lead to further dialectic progress. By means of the dialectic, Marx had declared that the workers had nothing to lose but their chains.

Inheriting the mantle of leadership from Marx, in 1903 Lenin created bolshevism when he falsely declared the men of his party faction to be of the majority, the Bolsheviks, and the opposing faction to be of the minority, the Mensheviks. In 1917 Lenin led the Bolsheviks in the Great October Revolution, and Russia became the world's first Communist-Marxist state. Tirelessly Lenin advanced the dialectic: since the workers had already lost their chains, he murdered the tsar.

Later, when Lenin lay ill, he warned the Communist party against Comrade Stalin, the general secretary. In spite of this, Stalin inherited power, and he, too, quickly employed the critical dialectic by declaring that Lenin had bequeathed the Marxist-Leninist-Bolshevik legacy to him.

As Lenin's Bolshevik heir, Stalin continued the development of the critical dialectic; since the workers no longer had chains and the tsar had been murdered, Stalin demonstrated the virtues of a classless society: absolutely everyone except Stalin could be the enemy. Even the party itself was subject to bloody purges. As for the workers, Stalin imprisoned, tortured, and murdered them, and he did this in numbers that the tsar had never dreamed of, because with the critical dialectic, progress knew no limits!

By contrast, the Krimsker Rebbe's only daughter, Rachel Leah Finebaum, knew very specific limits. In Moscow she lived in stagnant isolation in an armoire. Her husband, Hershel Shwartzman, a senior colonel in the Soviet secret police, the NKVD, did not have to be an expert practitioner of the critical dialectic to understand that the wife of his youth was quite literally the skeleton in his Marxist-Leninist-Bolshevik-Stalinist closet. And he knew about creating skeletons; Colonel Shwartzman worked to protect the world's most progressive revolution in the world's most Stalinist secret police prison, the Lubyanka.

The Lubyanka was both limited and limitless because of its sacred mission: to insure Stalinism. Like everything else in Stalin's Soviet Union, the Lubyanka had a past as well as a present. Under Stalin, either or both could prove to be liabilities. The Lubyanka's past certainly was an embarrassment, for it had been the home of a bourgeois insurance company.

CHAPTER ONE

WHO COULD DOUBT THE TRUTH OF SUCH A BUILDING? Certainly not Colonel Hershel Shwartzman! Inspiring confidence, symbolizing stability, the great massive structure had been the Rossiya—Russia Insurance Company. The Rossiya had successfully insured bourgeois lives against death, a mere physiological necessity, but eventually it failed; nothing could insure bourgeois life against a historical necessity, proletarian revolution. The tsarist Rossiya fell in a blaze of red glory to the Great October Revolution, but the imposing, massive edifice remained. Purged of its parasitic despoilers, it began a new life that only a revolution can bestow—and vigilantly served all the people in the noblest of pursuits, safeguarding the Communist revolution.

To compare the new Soviet workers' communal society with the preceding rotten exploitative capitalist one was an outrage. Where once there had been darkness, there was now light. How could one compare darkness and light? Aside from the moral travesty, it really was quite impossible. Still, if one were foolishly to risk such an absurd undertaking, one might suggest that the liberated building, now populated with the "new" Soviet man, continued to serve a remarkably similar function: insurance.

The Lubyanka actively insured the success of the world's only Communist revolution. It was busier than before and, understandably, more densely populated, for the Lubyanka was the secret police prison, the very home of the NKVD, the Soviet secret police. Of course it was busier: the tsarist Rossiya had to worry only about death, fire, flood, famine, and other natural events, but along with these insignificant occurrences, Stalin's protectors contended with Mensheviks, Trotskyites, kulaks, "former people" (tsarists), revisionists, anarchists, Social Revolutionaries, counterrevolutionaries, wreckers, double-dealers, saboteurs, spies of every ilk, engineers, all clerics, Ryutinists, fascists, right oppositionists, Bukharinists, left oppositionists, White Guards, capitalists, and most old Bolsheviks, to name a few.

All of these "unnatural" but cunning enemies were enmeshed in conspiracies, constantly hatching plots. And they were ubiquitous; they had even been unmasked posing as loyal party members. It was enough to make one's head spin, and NKVD colonel Hershel Shwartzman's had spun for the last several years. But now he was overwhelmed by it all. What had set his head turning most, however, weren't the frantic investigatory white-hot beams of NKVD light so much as the elusive shadow that played among them. That shadow was the staple of all insurance organizations: fear.

Fear had always made the denizens of the Lubyanka do strange things. Since the Lubyanka represented a progressive revolution, fear, too, had progressed; it caused the secret police officers themselves to do strange, unexpected things within the sheltering walls where Grisha Shwartzman now sat, facing a prisoner. Bourgeois insurance divided the risk, but Communist security multiplied the fear.

Never mind the fear, Grisha thought; but who could put that from his mind? It was always lurking like a shadow in the darkness. The light would shine, but there it would be, naked and ugly. Beyond the fear, the NKVD officer marveled; it was positively shameful! Grisha should have returned the prisoner to his cell almost two hours earlier. What was worse, he, an NKVD colonel, was permitting the prisoner to sleep. That was a scandal. Almost a sacrilege. When Colonel Hershel Shwartzman had taught interrogation, if a trained lieutenant so much as permitted a prisoner to close an eye, Grisha had mercilessly roasted the fledgling officer for lacking revolutionary vigilance. The officer never lacked it again; not if he wanted a real investigatory career in the NKVD. If not, let him guard convoys, administer camps, supervise institutions. There was more than enough to do, but if the cadet really wanted to protect the revolution by rooting out the evil that threatened to sap its lifeblood, he would listen.

Who could appreciate that lifeblood better than an old Chekist who had struggled to create the very revolution itself? The very first political institution created following the Great October Revolution was the Cheka—whose initials stood for Extraordinary All-Russian Commission of Struggle against Counterrevolution, Speculation, and Sabotage. Not until a month later did the party establish the Glorious Red Army under Trotsky, that traitor. There was a man who split the party and damaged the state! The

Chekists, however, were loyalty itself. The party's founder had enrolled Grisha in the fledgling organization. Oh, Grisha had taught them a thing or two. And now? Chekists themselves were not only suspect but even more suspect than anyone else. Why? Why those who had served so faithfully, the sword and shield of the revolution?

In the past few years, when his head had spun, Grisha had hoped that things would settle down and his head would cease to spin. Everything would fall into place and begin to make sense. He wanted to stifle the swirling chaos he was afflicted with—as a dizzy child reels, stumbling off a carousel—until little by little, the world would stop gyrating and once again only the carousel would revolve, balanced and bright, a large child's toy. Now Grisha realized there might be no climbing off the ever quickening machine. Disoriented, he would inevitably lose his grip and be flung off, to crash against stable objects such as the prison bars of the Lubyanka itself. Or worse, flung into the basement, where the dreaded pistol shots had no echoes.

Colonel Shwartzman had feared for the revolution; now he feared for his life. Others who had ridden the carousel more skillfully—moving to the very center, where the motion was negligible—had been thrown to their deaths. Henrik Yagoda, the chief of the NKVD, had disappeared. Grisha had not been allied with Yagoda; those who had, immediately followed the ex-chief into the basement. Until Yagoda's precipitous fall, Grisha had always assumed that he himself had an insurance policy against casualty. Grisha had served Stalin faithfully from the beginning. Not personally, but he had never made a secret of where his loyalties lay. After beloved Lenin's death, Grisha had understood that Stalin was the only man for the job. But look what had happened to Stalin's man, Yagoda. No, with Stalin there were no insurance policies, only sacrosanct areas where the NKVD would not arrest one of their own. The organs could never admit a mistake; therefore, no NKVD officer could ever be arrested while interrogating a prisoner. As long as the prisoner in front of him remained, Grisha was safe. Two hours ago he should have returned him to his cell. How much longer could he keep him here?

Grisha stared across his desk at his insurance. An experienced prisoner, the man sat erect. Anyone entering the office from behind would never suspect him of sleeping. His eyelids were inflamed and puffy from days without rest. Grisha guessed that his companion was about his own age, slightly over fifty, but the man had been in prison camps before he was returned to the Lubyanka, and he looked considerably older. For all the discomfort of the prisoner's predicament, his unguarded expression revealed something smug, as if the NKVD were not worth losing sleep over. Jealous that the man could rest so innocently, Grisha felt a rush of the old Chekist indignation at the prisoner's contempt for Soviet justice. A Chekist colonel had a sense of pride! Suddenly, Grisha went around the desk and kicked the prisoner in the shin. The man's eyes popped open, and he instinctively began to rub his leg.

"Mock Soviet justice!" Grisha cried indignantly. He wasn't acting. He felt the burning hatred welling up within him as if he had swallowed hot lead.

"We know everything. We know everything about you," Grisha railed. "You!" He wanted to spit out the prisoner's name, as if even pronouncing it left a bad taste in a decent man's mouth, but for the life of him he couldn't remember. He wanted to check the name on the folder lying on his desk, but he thought better of it. The organs were infallible and omniscient.

"You Trotskyite wrecker!" He uttered these words with the abhorrent loathing he felt for all those who had followed that arrogant theoretician. Stalin had gotten that right!

The prisoner looked slightly bewildered. Grisha had caught him with his guard down. Now was the time to press the advantage.

"Do you still deny it?" Grisha snarled.

Perplexed, the prisoner shifted his weight.

"Answer me," Grisha demanded.

"It's not true," the man said in simple honesty and looked strangely at his NKVD antagonist.

Offended, Grisha could see that the man was not the least bit intimidated.

"How can you expect me to believe that?" He twisted his face into a pained expression.

The prisoner began to answer, then hesitated, as if he thought better of it.

"Tell me," Grisha coaxed with a certain gruff sincerity. "We're here to tell the truth."

"For the last week you have been accusing me of Menshevik wrecking through Bukharinist counterrevolutionary circles," the man said with no emotion.

Shamed at his lack of revolutionary vigilance and enraged by the prisoner's lack of fear, Grisha screamed, "I'll squeeze your balls until you piss blood! You'll sign whatever the charge is. And if the charge changes, you'll sign again. You think it makes a difference. You'll sign that your mother was a garbage truck. And it will be true, too!"

Grisha's head was reeling. He had never talked this way. This was the new way, the way his younger colleagues spoke, all vulgar bluster. Ashamed of indulging in such a primitive outburst, and embarrassed—the organs never made a mistake—Grisha wanted to get rid of the prisoner immediately. He rang for the guard to remove him.

While waiting, he took his pen and entered a few meaningless remarks in the file about "double-dealing as a means of wrecking the truth." He didn't want to look at the prisoner until the guard arrived. Grisha wasn't afraid of revealing his own fear, but he was unnerved by the absence of any in the prisoner. The man should have experienced a terrible, debilitating fear that would reduce him to putty in the interrogator's hands, to be molded for the good of the state. Why wasn't he afraid? After all, Grisha really could squeeze his balls until he pissed blood. There were investigators in the building who beat prisoners on the base of their spines until they were crippled, and in some cases without the subtle pretense of serial blows. They simply snapped men's spines. Grisha's vulgar, demeaning threat might have been proved idle, but how could the prisoner, whatever his name was, know that? Grisha felt the shadow of his immediate superior Colonel Nikolai Svetkov hovering over him. Only Svetkov's informer would have nothing to fear. If Grisha popped this old Menshevik into a punishment cell for a week, he might look at things a little differently, but to do so would be admitting his own failure.

Grisha felt weak and vulnerable, which was the best reason not to put this what's-his-name into solitary. If he were in the hold, Grisha would be freed for another insulting assignment. Heaven only knew what Svetkov would come up with next time. In 1936, where in the world had he found a Menshevik? Grisha was probably better off with the case he had, embarrassing as it was. In the early twenties the Mensheviks had been jailed, and by the early thirties most had been exterminated. How could Svetkov swirl in from Kiev to Moscow and find a Menshevik to investigate?

Svetkov's handing the assignment to a colonel was a clear insult. "This calls for the tested eye of an old Chekist," Svetkov had announced with his usual burst of energy. It wasn't clear, however, who was testing whom. And as Grisha heard the guard approaching, he had an overwhelming desire not to be found wanting. Contradicting all his previous thoughts, he had what seemed to be a brilliant solution: he would send the leftover prisoner to a punishment cell for insulting Soviet justice. Yes, in a feverish rush he decided that was the certain way to save himself. It would demonstrate his loyalty, his courage, and the correctness of his beliefs. But another voice screamed that it would leave him naked, exposed to Svetkov's machinations and charges of incompetence. Svetkov would suggest that he had failed by not eliciting a confession from what's-his-name and by wasting a punishment cell that was needed for really dangerous elements. And if Svetkov could find a Menshevik with whom to torture him, what else might he find?

A knock on the door, and two guards entered. Grisha was swept by a wave of terror as the carousel whirled around. So they had come for him, too. Would his last ride be an elevator descent to the basement or a sedan drive to some NKVD woods outside the capital? As his mind split, falling into the basement and flitting to the outskirts of Moscow, his eyes fell onto the ugly, scratched surface of the blocky desk, and the filthy top suddenly fascinated him, with its myriad scratches, abrasions, and dirt; it was altogether unique and worth a lifetime of study. A lifetime he no longer possessed.

While Grisha studied the desk, one guard escorted the Menshevik from the office. The other stepped forward and cleared his throat. Reluctantly, Grisha looked up to discover that his jailer was Yuri, a plodding, dull-witted man whom he had gotten to know well over the past years. He lacked all personal spite, and Grisha looked at him in resignation.

"Colonel Svetkov would like to see you in his office now," Yuri announced.

"Why didn't he telephone?" Grisha asked suspiciously.

Yuri shrugged uncomfortably. It wasn't his job to guess why the new director of investigations did things the way he did. His job was to lock and unlock cells. He shrugged again.

"Who asked you to call me?" Grisha asked.

"The colonel himself," the guard answered.

"Where were you?" Grisha covered his embarrassment with a strong aggressive tone. No longer servile, he fixed his strong gaze on the jailer.

"In his office," the man replied, his discomfort steadily increasing.

"Good, Sergeant, things are working well. The party is doing its job!" Grisha announced with revolutionary bravado.

"Yes, Comrade Colonel," the guard replied with a serious enthusiasm that erased all signs of unease.

Grisha nodded, dismissing him. Comforted by the familiar dogma, Yuri left.

Grisha did not share the dullard's sense of well-being. What did Svetkov want, and why hadn't he used the telephone? Grisha didn't like it. Since he had arrived from Kiev two months ago, Svetkov had been working to isolate Grisha and discredit him. Take this Menshevik, this what's-his-name—and Grisha felt a pang of conscience. An NKVD investigator who spent five nights interrogating a socially hostile element and couldn't remember a name, or even the action of the enemy, discredited himself and should be isolated.

Colonel Shwartzman leaned forward and checked the front of the folder: Sergei Gasparov. Grisha quietly stared at the unfamiliar name. What was it?—a name on a folder in the Lubyanka, a paper tombstone. Grisha shook his head. A Menshevik. Who would have imagined such a thing these days? Realizing that the Mensheviks lacked all understanding of historical necessity and were bourgeois to the core, Lenin himself had begun to root them out. How could Grisha expect to remember a Menshevik? But Grisha couldn't forget Sergei Gasparov's eyes; they revealed no fear. A Menshevik buried alive. How could he not be afraid? His absence made Grisha uncomfortable—he no longer had an insurance policy. He picked up the folder and stood up. His superior, Nikolai Svetkov, wanted to see him.

CHAPTER TWO

Nikolai Svetkov's uncouth, bestial energy flowed out through the open office door. Grisha could hear the animated, shouting voice and sensed the appearance of the speaker. Ruddy, thick Russian features crowded onto an insufficient expanse of face. Unkempt, his rumpled tunic would be hanging like a shaggy coat. He often draped it over his chair to reveal a smudged shirt badly in need of a wash; his shirttails, like dark, dirty rain clouds, ballooned out of pants inevitably in need of pressing. Had Grisha learned that Svetkov, like the prisoners, slept in his clothes, he would not have been surprised.

The similarity to prisoners did not end there. Although both dreamed prolifically, good and bad dreams, Svetkov's were the prisoners' nightmares, whereas the prisoners' dreams were the chief investigator's nightmares. Indulging his rapaciousness, Svetkov seemed to thrive on the dark intimacy of his relationship to the prisoners. He always looked happy and prosperously well fed. There was a softness to his pink flesh, but Grisha didn't doubt the strength in the sturdy frame. Indeed, the apparent softness gave the false impression of greater bulk. The boorish, joking self-aggrandizement disguised an untrained but clever, perceptive mind. Like Stalin himself, Svetkov was most dangerous when he was most clownish, as if his laughter unleashed within him something terrible and capricious.

For all his fear of the speaker, Grisha wasn't listening to the bullying voice inside the office. He had been surprised to find a new secretary. The young, uniformed female officer invited Grisha to enter with a curt nod. Her hair was cut so short that it barely moved when she flipped her head. Although she hadn't been there the day before, she seemed to know who he was and acted with an arrogant confidence that Grisha envied. Yes, that's how it should be done! That's how he, too, had done it once—when he and the revolution were both young and glorious. But Chekist women had never been this mannish. Certainly not Maya Kirsanova; for all her severity and dedication, a few long blond hairs had always escaped the discipline of the tightly tied bun. Grisha found nothing astray on the new secretary. Nodding vigorously for him to enter the office, she seemed oddly sexless. Grisha straightened up, smoothed his neat tunic, and stepped into the large, impressive chamber.

Occupied with the telephone, Svetkov waved him gleefully inside, inviting him with a conspiratorial wink to appreciate his performance. Although he was grinning broadly, his voice was harsh and threatening when he spoke into the telephone.

"Oh, I'm sure you'll find a train, because if you don't, we'll have to march them over and dispose of them in your office. You leave us no choice!"

He paused while the party on the other end trembled in terror.

"I *know* you understand!" Svetkov bullied. He hung up the phone, turning to his live audience for approval.

On the couch sat Pechko, a junior lieutenant, who chuckled out loud at his commander's wit. One of the new men, Pechko had been introduced shortly before Svetkov's arrival. Grisha wanted to join in the laughter, but he felt too weary and too fearful that he might be among those marched off for disposal. Realizing that he couldn't ignore the joke without offending Svetkov, Grisha nodded wearily in agreement. "Yes, you won't find a larger office in Moscow than the stationmaster's."

Out of the corner of his eye, Grisha saw Pechko slyly examining Svetkov for the proper response. No sooner did the NKVD chief of investigations beam his approval and begin to guffaw than Pechko nodded vigorously and returned to chuckling. Grisha felt as if he were among idiots—rather boorish ones, too. But instantly Svetkov turned completely serious and motioned him to be seated. The man could switch gears with lightning speed. It made him all the more dangerous. Grisha took a seat in one of the frayed, overstuffed leather armchairs in front of the massive desk, which had once insured an empire. Like a drunk encountering a policeman, Pechko was trying to regain his sobriety; his unsuccessful attempts made him all the more ludicrous. Grisha focused on Svetkov.

"Pechko needs some information for his investigation," Svetkov was saying.

Grisha nodded agreeably. This was how the service was supposed to function. He pivoted slightly to face the junior lieutenant, who was seated on the large couch off to the side.

"What do you know about the Jewish New Year?" Pechko asked.

It was such a surprising question that Grisha wasn't sure he had understood correctly. In fact, he was certain that he had not. He stared in dull amazement at his questioner.

"The Jewish New Year," Pechko muttered with slight embarrassment.

"The Jewish New Year?" Grisha repeated, wondering why Pechko should be mentioning such a thing in the office of the director of investigations.

"Yes." Pechko nodded, a touch too aggressively.

"What about it?" Grisha asked.

"That's what I want to know," Pechko agreed.

"Why?" Grisha asked, befuddled and anxious.

"Why do you think! Because he has an investigation with a fanatic Jew!" Svetkov burst impatiently into their conversation.

Welcoming the interjection, Pechko nodded vigorously.

Grisha, too, had been recalled to his senses.

"Major Feldman handles religion. He's very knowledgeable," he informed them.

"Yes, we know, but we're *asking you,*" Svetkov said bluntly.

Grisha knew that he must not give in to an investigator. The first reasonable admission always opened a floodgate of demands and accusations. "Why?" he responded with equal bluntness.

"Because Feldman's not here, and you are," Svetkov replied.

"Where is he?"

"Major Feldman can't be everywhere. That's why all of us are here to help him," Svetkov announced sarcastically, with a shrug of disbelief at Grisha's unreasonable hostility.

Grisha sensed that he was making a fool of himself by standing on ceremony.

"What do you want to know?" he asked defensively, knowing that the game was already lost. You couldn't begin to cooperate and stop when you wanted to stop.

"Good," Svetkov said buoyantly, his overlarge mouth curving into a buffoonish grin. "After all, we're here to tell the truth," he laughed, burlesquing the NKVD line fed to all prisoners until they agreed to absolute untruths.

Pechko laughed dutifully, but Grisha did not. It was all he could do to keep from wincing. Svetkov glanced at Pechko, who quietly controlled himself.

"I have an old-fashioned Jew, a long coat and beard. Primarily a British spy, but he also committed economic sabotage. He's shaky, and I want the names of the other bloodsucking profiteers. Is there any way I can use the Jewish holy day to get him to tell the truth?"

"I don't really see what we could do in the Lubyanka," Grisha answered thoughtfully. After all, the Lubyanka was not a synagogue, was it?

"What do these Jews do on their New Year?" Svetkov asked directly.

No, Grisha didn't like it, but he began to concentrate on Rosh Hashanah for the first time in many years. "It's the beginning of the New Year. It's the day of judgment for the coming year. In the synagogue they pray, and at home they dip bread and apples into honey for a sweet year. It's a holiday, but a serious one," Grisha concluded with a certain vagueness concerning events deeply buried under the weight of decades. He felt that he was omitting something important, but couldn't imagine what that might be.

"What about special wine? Do they use a special wine?" Pechko asked.

"No, I don't think they do. They use the wine they always do," Grisha answered.

"What wine is that?"

"Jewish wine. They make it themselves. I suppose it is special to them, if that's what you mean, but it's the same wine they use all year for religious blessings."

"What do you think of Pechko letting the prisoner have some in his office to celebrate the New Year?" Svetkov proposed.

"To create dependence and the belief that I really do want to help him," Pechko encouraged by way of explanation.

Grisha couldn't help raising his eyebrows in puritanical disapproval.

"You don't think it's a good idea?" Svetkov asked.

"Who needs bourgeois superstition? We have our own Bolshevik methods, and they have been proven effective," he answered forcefully.

Pechko glanced at Svetkov; both looked slightly disappointed.

"I suppose so," Svetkov said.

"I'll continue then with the usual method tonight?" Pechko asked his superior.

"Did you know that tonight is the Jewish New Year?" Svetkov asked Grisha.

In spite of Svetkov's barbed question, Grisha merely shook his head. There was something special about Rosh Hashanah that he was forgetting. "Oh," he announced, like a schoolboy recalling the right answer, "they blow a ram's horn."

"Why do they do that?" Svetkov asked curiously.

"They think it helps them to become better people."

"Does it?" Svetkov asked seriously.

"How should I know?" Grisha snapped.

"Your father might have told you," Svetkov suggested casually.

"My father died when I was an infant."

"Maybe your father-in-law, the grand rabbi in America, might have told you, or his daughter, Rachel Leah, your dear wife, might have mentioned it this morning," Svetkov speculated.

Grisha was surprised that this insult wasn't delivered with Svetkov's usual obscene smile.

"If anyone did, I don't remember," he responded.

"Some things are best forgotten," Svetkov said sympathetically.

Grisha squirmed uncomfortably before this new, considerate Svetkov.

"What should I do with the wine?" Pechko asked petulantly, now that he wasn't permitted to serve it to his prisoner.

An extraordinary grin wreathed Svetkov's face. "Give it to me. Tonight is the Jewish New Year. I'll know what to do with it." He laughed.

Pechko, slightly confused, was trying to laugh when Svetkov's face contracted. "That's enough of this nonsense,

Pechko. Get back to work. Colonel Shwartzman and I have some serious matters to discuss."

Under Svetkov's disapproving gaze Pechko aborted his laugh with two deep choking breaths and rose to leave. Beneath the chandelier he bowed awkwardly toward his superiors and, breathing unevenly, marched self-consciously out of the room, closing the door behind him.

Turning to Grisha, Svetkov remained serious, but softened his expression as if he were dealing with a respected comrade. "Colonel, forget that silliness. A simple problem needed a simple solution. I called you in for something really very important." Svetkov paused, as if searching for the right words. "Some cases are so delicate"—the word seemed to discomfort him—"that only the most senior investigators can be trusted with them. It's no secret that no one here has had your experience defending the revolution. We are relying on you to make use of that formidable experience. This is a case that demands an old Chekist. Unfortunately, we have only one left." Svetkov delivered his charge and sat back with evident relief.

Stimulated and flattered by Svetkov's appeal—he had never known him to be so respectful for so long—Grisha sat up straighter to receive the particulars. Svetkov, however, said no more. He simply sat back and nodded very soberly, as if he had already delivered all the details.

"How long has the case been under investigation?" Grisha asked.

"A few days. It was entrusted directly to me, and I am giving it straight to you to handle," Svetkov answered and again fell back into his chair.

"Perhaps we should start with the file," Grisha suggested.

"There isn't any," Svetkov answered.

Although Svetkov remained silent, Grisha looked at him for an explanation.

"It is that delicate," Svetkov explained.

"Then how do I proceed?"

"The prisoner himself will explain everything." Svetkov seemed nervous and frightened by the case, but Grisha felt the thrill of a formidable challenge.

"When do we start?"

"In a few minutes he will be brought here," Svetkov answered.

"Here?"

"This demands the strictest secrecy. You will use my office with all its resources at your disposal. Needless to say, you will be relieved of all other duties until this business is completed."

Svetkov rose from his chair and made a few haphazard attempts to stuff his billowing shirttails into his pants. These unsuccessful thrusts merely flattened the dirty garment against his body. Removing the tunic that he had been wrinkling with his own bulk from the back of his chair, he put it on. Svetkov even made an effort to brush his hair with his hand.

Grisha wondered what prisoner could elicit such respect from Svetkov.

"Sit here behind the desk. It wouldn't make sense otherwise," he suggested.

Grisha rose and took the seat of Svetkov, chief of the Lubyanka. As he passed his nominal superior, he was surprised to find that the man was sweating.

"Whatever you need, Tatiana will get for you. She is a

good girl. Thoroughly reliable. She has been briefed as to the investigation, but she knows nothing of the case itself. Are you ready?"

"Yes," Grisha answered.

"Then have her send him in."

Grisha picked up the phone and heard the severe, efficient "Yes?" of the new NKVD secretary.

"Send him in," Grisha commanded crisply.

Svetkov crossed the large office as if on his way to escape. For a moment, the insane thought crossed Grisha's mind that they were going to assassinate him seated at the desk of the chief of investigations. Instead the door opened and a guard entered, followed by a man sandwiched between him and another guard. Svetkov nodded. The first guard stopped, permitting the prisoner to enter. A look of loathing on his exaggerated features, Svetkov let the man walk by him and quickly exited, as if he were escaping a foul odor. The guard stood at attention to Svetkov, then quickly followed him out, closing the door.

Grisha sat up straight, focusing intently on the man who had just been deposited in front of him. After staring several moments to be certain, he was indeed surprised.

CHAPTER THREE

WHEN GRISHA TOOK SVETKOV'S SEAT BEHIND THE DRAB, massive desk, he felt a resurgence of the revolutionary enthusiasm that had once pulsed routinely through his Chekist veins. More importantly, he felt a purity of purpose that he had not experienced for several long, disappointing years. He smoothed his tunic as if it were a priestly vestment and he the priest who must assure the sanctity of the service. So much wasn't right, but now that the Communist party had chosen him to protect its inner core, there was hope. From this bleak office in the Lubyanka would radiate a new vigilance that would cut away the smothering calcification and expose the life-generating marrow. Mankind's confidence in the Great October Revolution would be justified!

Grisha sat in the seat of power with a revolutionary confidence that he represented the forces of progress. Historical necessity tickled him like a feather, and he wanted to laugh aloud. Yes, and he had not arrived a moment too soon. Careerists, opportunists, apparatchiks, were trampling the revolutionary flame into the dust; fear of his own arrest was sufficient proof that things were in a terrible state! But the pure spark that had ignited the revolution had survived and would be fanned into flame anew, igniting, illuminating, warning, tempering, and spreading.

Grisha's inspired mind leaped to the battlements of the Kremlin for a historical perspective. Only an old Chekist could retrieve the Great October Revolution. "What's to Be Done?" Lenin had heralded, and Grisha knew. The party had to retrace its steps to that point where it had taken the wrong path and from there proceed along the proper way with Bolshevik confidence. The revolution had gone wrong with Trotsky. Exiling the traitor had not solved the problem, but miraculously, that moment could be recaptured. If not the moment, then the man himself; and through the man, things could be set right. Perhaps Trotsky had returned to Russia on his own to help solve the problems he had caused, but Grisha doubted it. An arrogance such as that could not admit error.

No, Trotsky must have been captured and spirited back to Russia. Stalin himself must have understood, for only the general secretary had the authority to give such an order. It would be Grisha's job to see that the prisoner cooperated. If he did, then the real counterrevolutionaries could be rooted out. As to the personal future of the prisoner, Stalin no doubt would want him shot. There was certainly something to be said for that, especially if it meant that others wouldn't be shot, but even that might be unnecessary if he confessed properly. After all those years of promising prisoners that if they told the truth, they would have nothing to fear, such might really be the case!

The thought stimulated Grisha; it would justify so much that had happened; so much that he had done to so many. That the "old man" could become the "new man" excited him further. Thus freed from his havoc-wreaking attempts to create a new man, Comrade Stalin could return to building the country, the job he was suited for. But Grisha restrained his enthusiasm; all of this was in the future. First he had to gain the cooperation of the party's most brilliant theoretician and most dangerous enemy. A man who had created and commanded the Red Army. Whose case could be more delicate than this, a case so delicate that as yet no file existed?

After Svetkov and the guard had departed, Grisha gazed steadily at the prisoner. He was, indeed, surprised.

"Lev Davidovich?" Grisha called softly across the large chamber, using Trotsky's first name and patronymic, informal name, in faint hope that his disappointment was premature.

Accepting Grisha's gentle, indistinct query as an invitation, the prisoner stepped humbly forward to be able to hear better. Although he said nothing, his pale meek face silently drew itself into an apology. "Yes?" it seemed to ask in reluctant embarrassment.

This pained, vulnerable attitude momentarily disarmed Grisha.

"You're not Leon Trotsky?" Grisha uttered disconsolately.

"No." The prisoner responded so softly that Grisha couldn't hear him, but he could see the man shaking his head in humiliation that he had disappointed once again.

The prisoner's extraordinary humility saved Grisha

from the collapse of his own exuberant expectations of interrogating Trotsky. Grisha experienced surprise and disappointment, but almost no embarrassment before this new prisoner, who seemed to lack any defiance or mistrust. The man even seemed somewhat relieved to find himself standing across from the NKVD director of investigations.

"Sit down," Grisha said, not uncharitably, and the man responded quickly but with slow, careful movements. The effect was strange and further aroused Grisha's interest. The man seemed to be in good health. There were no signs that he had been beaten. He wore his belt and shoelaces. Obviously, he had not been processed as a formal prisoner. Grisha assumed that he was being held in one of the special cells where accommodations and diet were more like those of a comfortable hotel than a prison.

And yet, as frightened as the man was, he didn't seem afraid so much of Grisha as of himself. He seemed to look to the NKVD officer for help, but without the usual righteous indignation of the innocent. The man had an aura of self-professed guilt about him. His strange eyes trumpeted it. They were preternaturally large and filled with both shame and innocence. Where had Grisha seen something like this—the pale, wide eyes, the slow movements, the innocent fear and complete vulnerability? He was reminded of the small, furry creatures of the night, who lived in the treetops and relied on their large eyes and inaccessible habitat to survive. Once an adversary discovered them, they were helpless. At the zoo, Grisha had liked them at once. And only them. Tigers, snakes, crocodiles, he had recognized them all as enemies of the revolution. On battlefronts and in interrogation rooms he had struggled against their counterrevolutionary claws, poison, sharp teeth, and voracious jaws. At the zoological garden, Grisha was fascinated but tense. He knew them all from the cages of the Lubyanka—beasts whose very nature was to prey upon the Great October Revolution. He always insisted that his cadets spend time in serious study at the zoo. The grasping, scampering monkeys, shameless profiteers and speculators. The kulak birds sang so beautifully but were the first to steal grain from another's harvest. And the ugly nonparty owls, sleeping by day and screeching by night. A comrade could learn a lot from the brutal world of nature, all right. But one creature always drew him to its cage in wonderment. He had seen them all before in the Lubyanka except for the large-eyed, slow-moving, nocturnal lemur. Fearful and trusting, an investigator's dream.

"You are?" Grisha inquired imperiously.

"Dmitri Cherbyshev," the man answered meekly.

"Would you like to tell me in your own words why you're here?" Grisha asked. Stressing "in your own words" suggested clearly that the NKVD interrogator most certainly knew all and was merely being kind.

The prisoner's large eyes filled with a fright and a horror that threatened to paralyze him. Although the eyes did not close in the least, they no longer focused on the questioner. The effect was as if out of embarrassment the prisoner had looked away or lowered his glance. Had he done so, Grisha would have been offended and doggedly pursued the prisoner. This strange inward retreat, however, did not offend Soviet justice. Grisha was reminded of Svetkov's term "delicate." Here was an extremely delicate prisoner. Sensitive to the man's plight, Grisha sat up attentively.

"It's difficult, isn't it?" Grisha suggested sympathetically.

The prisoner looked at his NKVD interrogator and nodded. Although Grisha didn't think the man would burst into tears—the wide eyes seemed beyond tears—Grisha was concerned that the man might sink within their wet white surface as if into a moist fog.

"I understand," Grisha said with studied sincerity. "Perhaps I was a little too sudden. I can see that you want to tell the truth, don't you?"

Dmitri glanced at Grisha and nodded.

"Sometimes it's not easy. We understand that, but it's always the best way. It's the only way. After all, we're here to help you. Maybe we should get to know one another. Why don't you tell me a little bit about yourself. Dmitri, where do you work?"

Dmitri's eyes focused. "At the Lenin Library," he said.

"That's a wonderful place to work. A wonderful name, too. Of course, with my activities here, I just don't have the time to visit it the way I would like to. It's one of the world's largest collections, isn't it?"

The prisoner merely nodded.

"What do you do there?" Grisha asked buoyantly.

"I am in charge of some of the foreign collections," Dmitri answered.

"What foreign languages do you know?" Grisha inquired.

"Polish, English, French, German—all rather well, and I read several others," the prisoner answered simply.

"You're obviously very talented," Grisha commented respectfully. "Do you enjoy your work, Dmitri?"

Dmitri squirmed uncomfortably in the large leather armchair without being able to formulate an answer.

"You don't enjoy your work?" Grisha suggested.

"I don't know."

"Why not?" Grisha asked politely.

Dmitri looked at Grisha. "Since I've had these difficulties, I just don't know."

The man put his hand to his forehead in desperation and shook his head. Grisha was sure now that he was about to cry.

"Would you like a drink of water?" he suggested.

The man removed his hand from his head and fell back into the deep upholstered leather chair, gripping the armrests. Grisha picked up the phone and heard the new secretary's crisp "Yes?"

"May we have a pitcher of water, please?" The voice responded, "Immediately," and Grisha regretted not having been more imperious in his order. She probably would have respected him more if he hadn't said please. That's not the way things used to be.

"Where do you live?"

"In the Arbat. Close to the library," he answered.

Grisha nodded. "Married?"

The prisoner shook his head. Grisha thought he detected a telltale sign of guilt.

"Have you been married?" he asked casually.

Again Dmitri shook his head with the same telltale signs.

"Engaged?"

A third time the prisoner shook his head. The fact was that this timid Dmitri didn't look like a ladies' man, but the Cheka had been fooled often enough on that score. Even after the revolution, sex remained a mystery. Somewhere in Moscow there must be a woman who would thrill to Dmitri Cherbyshev's wide, frightened eyes and clutch him close. Not that much would happen between them with the man's debilitating fear, but then, Grisha thought, who knows; there seem to be enough of those frightened furry little lemurs to populate the jungle and the zoos, too.

A knock on the door interrupted his thoughts. He buzzed Tatiana in. She entered with a tray containing a large, heavy cut-glass pitcher and two heavy glasses. Grisha had seen them before in this office, but he wondered anew whether they weren't left from tsarist times. Still, he couldn't imagine that glassware could survive so long anywhere in Bolshevik Russia, especially in the Lubyanka, where things were destined to be broken. Imperiously he raised his arm and silently pointed to the portion of the desk directly in front of the prisoner. Tatiana primly put the tray down and turned to leave.

Grisha watched her mannish walk, all shoulders and arms, no hips at all. Who would find anything like that attractive? Maya Kirsanova came to mind. She had Bolshevik steel in her heart, but she had hips and human needs, too. If Grisha had had a revolutionary love, she was it. Should he have divorced and married her? There was no great romantic love, but politically Maya was aware, a trusted party member, and there was grace in their relationship. The Cossacks had chided him about it, but with respectful affection. He had envied the natural way they sat on their horses, and they had envied him. They were right, too. He and Maya had "ridden" with a natural physical dignity that made them both proud and grateful to have one another. But this stern, short-haired NKVD secretary—

who could ride her with any joy? What would the Cossacks have thought of her? They most probably would have compared her to a mule instead of a graceful, thin-faced mare or a strong, supple Maya Kirsanova.

My heavens, he had let her go! And why was he thinking of her now? Since Kirov had been shot, no one seemed to be screwing in Russia anymore. If they were, the NKVD would know about it, and the NKVD didn't know about it, so it must not be happening. In the purges one-fourth of Leningrad had disappeared. Who could make love waiting for a knock on the door? Grisha couldn't; he knew that. So what difference did it make if Chekist women no longer existed? Neither did the Cheka, and neither did sex. Why was he sitting at Svetkov's desk and in his leather chair with such thoughts and such tense discomfort?

"Dmitri, it's a little warm in here. Why don't you have a drink?" Grisha suggested. Welcoming the chance to get up from the chair, he poured the man a glass of water.

Dmitri, relieved at the opportunity to do something with his trembling hand, took it. Grisha watched the water roll about in frenzy as Dmitri's spasmodic anxiety entered the liquid. A quick darting wave roiled forward and leaped over the rim, running down onto Dmitri's hand. He leaned forward, licking at his thumbs with the same slow grace that had marked his entry, and then, surprisingly, his hands ceased to shake. He sipped from the glass and rested it on the desk.

"Thank you," he said with cringing sincerity.

Eager to begin, Grisha returned to Svetkov's seat.

"Dmitri, take another drink," he suggested.

Obsequiously, Dmitri obeyed.

"You know we're here to tell the truth. Sometimes what we have to say is difficult or painful. Sometimes we are ashamed of the things we have done, but there is nothing better for us than the truth. Often we imagine that some things are frightening to tell, but they generally reveal themselves as not half so bad as we imagine. And you'll feel better for having told the truth, too. I can see that you aren't very comfortable now. Am I right, Dmitri?"

Dmitri nodded.

"Remember, we're all here in this building to protect you, because when we protect the revolution, we are protecting all of us, aren't we?"

Again Dmitri nodded, but this time in a curt, perfunctory manner.

"So why don't we just start at the beginning," Grisha coaxed.

Dmitri nodded and then reached to drink from his glass. Instead of the usual timid sip, he took two long gulps that almost drained the large tumbler. He grasped the glass tightly, his fingers blanching white, and his great fearful eyes swam in frenzy as if they were drowning in the copious fluid he had swallowed. Suddenly his lips began moving. Staring at the floor, he spoke so softly that at first Grisha wasn't aware that he was talking. After several sentences he stopped. Although Grisha had not heard a word, he thought it best to be encouraging.

"Now that wasn't so bad, was it?" Grisha asked. Without waiting for an answer, he continued. "It never is. It's our imagination that is the problem."

"Yes, but what can we do about it?" Dmitri asked. His face wore a look of supplication.

"Tell the truth," Grisha stated triumphantly.

"And that will control our imagination?" Dmitri countered doubtfully.

Dmitri clearly thought that he, Grisha, had heard his confession. Grisha thought it better not to reveal the truth to him now. After all, there were lesser and greater truths, *istina* and *pravda*. *Pravda* was the very newspaper of the party, and only the party could determine the greater truth, the revolutionary truth. How could he begin to explain that to a nonparty person, and such a troubled one at that?

"Of course the truth will help control the imagination. If necessary, the truth can even spark the revolutionary imagination. Lenin first imagined the revolution, didn't he? And Stalin imagined the new man."

Grisha had added the latter for good form, but he noticed that the prisoner shrank back in horror.

Embarrassed at his ignorance and frustrated by the failure of his gentle technique, Grisha asked abruptly, "When did all this begin?"

The prisoner's lips began to move.

"I can't hear a word you are saying. You'll have to speak louder," Grisha announced.

"I'm sorry," Dmitri said softly, but loud enough for Grisha to hear.

"That's better. Now, my friend, when did all this trouble begin?"

"I think after Kirov, the Leningrad party chairman, was shot," he answered.

Here at last was something Grisha could sink his teeth into. Stalin himself had rushed to Leningrad to investigate the murder of the second most important Communist.

"Were you in Leningrad at the time?" Grisha asked. Dmitri shook his head. "Did you know the assassin, Leonid Nikolayev?" A shake of the head in reply. "Were you involved with the desperate Zinovievite circles that manipulated Nikolayev?" Another negative response. "The White Guards, then?" A shake of the head. "Trotskyite?" Another no. "But you did welcome the Leningrad party chairman's murder?" Grisha accused with certainty.

"No," Dmitri murmured innocently, horrified at the suggestion.

"Why not?" Grisha asked, as if the prisoner had every reason to.

The question confused the prisoner. "No," he murmured. "I didn't know very much about Kirov. I should have known more. He was one of the party's most important leaders." His voice trailed off.

"In what way were you implicated in Kirov's death?" Grisha asked, slightly exasperated.

"In the way everyone was—a lack of vigilance and a lack of Communist awareness," the prisoner answered.

"And do you admit to this?" Grisha demanded.

"I thought everyone did. Only party members spoke at the meetings, and they said we were all responsible."

"These were meetings of the library staff?" Grisha asked. Dmitri nodded.

"And they began after Kirov's death?"

"No, we had them before, but they weren't so important. After Kirov's murder, we began having them regularly, every day for two weeks. Work at the library practically came to a halt. We met from the afternoon until the late evening. We learned about the murder and the threats to the state."

"And it was at one of these meetings that you admitted your betrayal?"

Dmitri shook his head.

"You didn't admit your betrayal?" Grisha asked reasonably.

Again Dmitri shook his head.

"What other possibility is there?" Grisha wondered affably. Without confirming or denying Grisha's rhetorical question, the prisoner sat staring at the NKVD officer. Grisha waited while a tremor of guilt played across the man's face like wind over water, then he asked gently, "Are you going to answer?"

Dmitri nodded. He looked as if something were stuck in his throat.

"I thought we agreed that you would feel better if you told the truth," Grisha gently reminded him.

"No one spoke except party members. They were very upset."

"At whom?"

"At everyone."

"At everyone?" Grisha asked incredulously.

"Not at Comrade Stalin himself. Comrade Stalin had relied on all of us, and we had all failed him. Enemies were everywhere, and we had to become more alert to these destroyers and wreckers," Dmitri recited by rote.

"You didn't believe it?" Grisha suggested.

"At first I didn't understand it. It seemed that Comrade Stalin could do everything alone if he had to, but that it would be so much better if we helped him," Dmitri explained in his usual timid manner. Then he fairly exploded, "They talked about Stalin all the time!"

"What were you hiding that you didn't think they should know?" Grisha queried.

The prisoner, however, paying no attention to Grisha, continued his narrative. "You couldn't help but think about Stalin. The more I listened to them, the more I thought about the general secretary. We were instructed to follow Stalin, even to anticipate his thoughts, but in fact it was only through Stalin that we could know what was right or wrong. I couldn't understand our relationship to him. He needed us, and he didn't need us. He loved us, and he hated us. I thought, What does he want from us? He wanted to be all things, but only to the parts of us he wanted. We were urged to think about the general secretary all the time."

Dmitri suddenly turned to Grisha. His impassioned eyes still held a full measure of fright.

"Do *you* understand?" he pleaded.

Grisha was afraid that he did.

"Everyone claims they don't. Even the psychiatrists. The NKVD ignored the letter I sent them. Do you *understand?*" Dmitri implored.

"Go on," Grisha ordered dryly, but with a scratchy voice that betrayed him.

Obsequious, almost sycophantic rapture shone through the frightened eyes. Grisha was worried that the man would say, "Good," for the prisoner knew that he understood. Grisha was thankful that the man merely nodded slightly and returned to his tale.

"You see, Stalin was the party. The party was the state.

The state was the people. So Stalin was us. But we weren't Stalin. How could mere little insects like us be Stalin? I admit the thought is preposterous. Poor Stalin had enemies everywhere. Not just in the wicked foreign capitals, not just in the old Russia. Stalin had an enemy in every one of us. These enemies permitted Kirov to be killed and by extension the party, and thereby Stalin himself. Stalin was building the new Soviet man, and we were trying to kill this new man. So of course he was angry. After all, hadn't we killed Kirov? And weren't we planning far worse acts against the Great Teacher Stalin himself?"

Here the prisoner paused.

"Were you?" Grisha asked gravely.

"How could I plot against Stalin? How could I plot against myself? How could I do such a thing?" the man fairly shouted in indignation.

He gripped the arms of the chair. His eyes burned with shame. "How could I do such a thing?" he repeated in quiet, amazed horror. His voice broke suddenly, the great open eyes blinked, and the man was crying.

Grisha pointed to the water pitcher, but the prisoner ignored the suggestion. He composed himself to continue. When he did so, it was in a calm, sober voice filled with all its former apology and embarrassment.

"I must admit that I had been warned, but I didn't listen. The party members warned us that it seemed easy, whereas in reality nothing was more difficult. They warned us that in our most unsuspecting moments we could fall prey to counterrevolutionary anti-Soviet activity. Do you know why I didn't listen?" He didn't wait for an answer. "I was bored. Everything was Stalin. Stalin this and Stalin that. These meetings became our primary work. We were to defend Stalin against everything. Politics didn't interest me. I barely knew who Kirov was. How could I join counterrevolutionary activity? What could I do? It all seemed so fantastic. It was fantastic, and of course they were right. I had been warned and—" The prisoner paused. "And as I told you, it happened. I admit it was my fault."

Not having heard the original confession, Grisha did not quite understand what this strange, bewildered, and bewildering man was supposed to have done.

"Let's go through it again. In detail," Grisha suggested.

"In detail?" the prisoner asked in revulsion.

"Yes, you seem to have found your tongue. We want to hear the truth, don't we?"

Grisha paused, but Dmitri simply stared across the great expanse of desk as if he were overlooking an abyss.

"And another thing. Don't lower your voice. You don't have to shout either. Just speak normally."

"May I have some more water?" the prisoner rasped. He sounded as if his tongue were sticking to his mouth.

"Yes, of course," Grisha said.

The man poured a large glassful and began to sip it, staring alternately into the disappearing fluid and at his NKVD officer.

"You didn't hear me the first time, did you?" Dmitri asked softly.

Embarrassed at being caught in his subterfuge, Grisha said noncommittally, "Just repeat it."

"They never do," the prisoner said. "No one ever has. I'm to blame. I always drop my voice in shame. It's not your fault."

Annoyed at the prisoner's arrogant attempt to exonerate him, Grisha said, "Speak up, please."

"I'll try," he whispered.

"Louder," Grisha ordered.

"Is this better?" the prisoner asked in a nearly normal speaking voice.

"Much," Grisha answered.

The prisoner nodded, but didn't continue speaking.

Grisha stifled his rising impatience. "I know it must be difficult, but I can assure you that you will feel better once you have told me the truth."

"I was always thinking about Stalin," the prisoner began quietly.

"Yes, I understand that," Grisha said patiently.

"Good. Most people don't. I'm not sure that I do. But I think my confusion began after what happened."

The prisoner was staring at his investigator. Grisha nodded.

"And every night I would find myself alone with him."

"You would go home and imagine that Comrade Stalin was in your living room?" Grisha asked.

"No," the prisoner answered, then added, "In the bedroom."

He stopped again, a mask of anguish on his face.

"What was the general secretary doing there?" Grisha wondered.

"He was with me. We were together . . ." The man's voice trailed off, then he closed his eyes and whispered, "like a man and a woman."

He opened his great fearful eyes to view the reaction. It was slow in coming.

"Like a man and woman?" Grisha repeated in prudish confusion.

"As much as such things are possible," the prisoner answered.

"Possible?" Grisha repeated uncertainly.

"Every night it's the same. There we are together like two creatures. One mounting the other from behind. Every night. Always the same."

He made this confession in horror, suffused with relief at having told the truth.

"This has been going on every night since Kirov was killed. You can't imagine what it is like to live with something like that," he added.

Grisha heard the man's relief at having confessed to the sword and shield of Soviet society, but he himself could not believe that he had heard it right.

"You and . . . the general secretary?" he said in a tone of revulsion.

"Yes," the prisoner said forthrightly, and in the rush of confession sought for greater clarity. "Like two dogs, one on the other. Every night. It's disgusting."

"Disgusting? It's revolting. It's filth!" Grisha was sincerely horrified.

"Yes, I know," the prisoner agreed shamefully.

In his puritanical revulsion, Grisha felt the carousel begin to turn. Slowly, ever so slowly at first, with no sense of motion as the machine slipped its brake. His first realization came as the background began sliding around. Grisha knew that soon the platform would gather speed and revolve with merciless rapidity. If only it could be stopped now. A case of mistaken identity. Grisha prayed for a simple case of mistaken identity.

"Are you sure?" he asked quickly.

"Yes, very," the prisoner insisted.

"No, I don't mean that. I mean the general secretary. Are you sure it was him?"

Dmitri looked confused. "Absolutely. His picture is everywhere."

"Yes, of course it is," Grisha frantically agreed. "But if"—he paused reflexively—"if you are down on all fours like a dog, how can you be sure who is on top? It could be anyone. You are facing the ground in front of you, and you can't see who is behind you. It might be anyone. That's so, isn't it?" he demanded triumphantly.

This brilliant analysis pained the prisoner but didn't lessen his certainty.

"Well, I suppose you're right about the person on the bottom if he doesn't turn around, but I'm always on top," he explained.

"You mean?" Grisha whispered in shock.

"I'm sorry, but I couldn't catch what you said," the prisoner apologized, sliding forward in his seat to hear better.

"You!" Grisha rasped, directing an accusing finger at his prisoner, "and . . ." his finger pointed down, indicating the party on the bottom whose exalted name he couldn't dare mention in such an inferior position.

"Yes, the general secretary is always on the bottom. He prefers it that way. I know, because when he does turn around, he is smiling."

The prisoner sat back in his armchair. Grisha, however,

moved forward to the edge of his. Feeling as if his head were going to explode, he grasped it on either side and pressed in on his temples. Through a haze of murky sensations—contempt for Svetkov, fear of Stalin, hatred of Trotsky—that began to swirl, he knew that only one preventive explosion might save him, his career, and his life. He pushed against his skull to compose himself, dropped his hands, sat up, and very deliberately unfastened his holster. Without removing his eyes from the prisoner, he drew his pistol. This time he did not place it on the desk. Releasing the safety, he continued to point the heavy weapon directly at the prisoner.

"Dreams are not permitted the new Soviet man. They cannot be controlled," he explained in a quiet, menacing voice. "They are inevitably insurrectional and anti-Soviet."

"Yes, I know." The prisoner confirmed the verdict.

As Dmitri Cherbyshev stared at the deadly, cocked weapon, his eyes widened in fearful vulnerability. Slowly they changed, and Grisha read in them no sense of outrage or desire to escape. Quivering slightly, Cherbyshev stared almost worshipfully at the instrument that would determine his fate. The gentle nocturnal lemur faced the sharp-toothed cat in daylight. Denizen of a nightmare world from which one could never wake up, he had only one hope, to stop dreaming. In the chamber of the automatic lay the dark, leaden release from his horrors.

The prisoner appealed to the NKVD officer to liberate him. It was an appeal that in most cases would have been immediately successful, but in the netherworld of the Lubyanka, a prisoner's wishes were rarely met—even when they coincided with those of the state security administration.

Otherwise, the terror would hardly be worthy of its name, and names were very important to the masters of the Lubyanka. Grisha, as Colonel Hershel Shwartzman, knew at once that his only chance to survive dictated that he march the prisoner off the rug onto the marble floor and blow his filthy anti-Soviet scheming brains out. Logic demanded it, and the NKVD colonel who held the pistol was not squeamish about executing such brutal logic. Grisha, however, was hesitant, for he did understand what even the Soviet psychiatrists refused to admit: Stalin had driven the man crazy. If Stalin were us, as Dmitri had said, then Grisha was Dmitri. Grisha chose not to shoot the prisoner, and thereby Colonel Shwartzman applied inadvertently an even more inspired principle of the Lubyanka: mercy can be the cruelest torture of all.

Grisha placed the exposed weapon on the desk and reached for a pen and several sheets of paper. He could see the great wave of disappointment flooding the prisoner's eyes. Colonel Shwartzman was determined to keep the prisoner from slipping below their surface.

"It won't take long. You understand that we must have a few particulars before we proceed."

The prisoner stirred, blinking his eyes as if at the gentler rays of daylight. When the colonel was certain that he had the man's attention, he gently patted his pistol.

"It won't go anywhere. I promise. I know what you want. Trust me," he said duplicitously.

The prisoner nodded. His eyes remained on the pistol. Colonel Shwartzman glanced down to straighten the several sheets he had placed one upon the other.

It seemed warmer, and although the colonel didn't

quite understand why, Grisha did: he felt the itch, not of historical necessity, but of burgeoning curiosity as to Dmitri Cherbyshev's filthy insurrectional activities. His other self, the colonel, stifled this interest as inappropriate. He, too, certainly shared it, but Grisha had sought refuge in the bureaucratic world of the colonel's NKVD. The normal operating procedure of the NKVD demanded a complete signed confession in accordance with Bolshevik methods that "have proven effective," as he had preached to Svetkov some time earlier.

CHAPTER FOUR

MARXISM, OR SCIENTIFIC SOCIALISM, AS MARX HIMSELF referred to it, was very much a child, albeit a radical one, of the Western tradition. Therefore the Marxist critical dialectic expressed a dynamic of change that was analytic, precise, intellectual, and moral. And just as the conservative Western tradition of governance had transferred sanctity from traditional divinity to secular constitution and law (even if these were only bourgeois legalisms), so, too, for supremely secular Leninist-Stalinist bolshevism, constitution and law were of paramount importance. Consequently, as bolshevism developed into lethal terror, Soviet law remained essential and became even more progressive.

No Bolshevik law had proven more effective than Article 58. Colonel Shwartzman, like all NKVD officers, felt a great fondness for all 140 articles of the Criminal Code of 1926, the great literary work of the revolution. Every opus has its special chapter, story, poem, psalm, or song that captures the human spirit and in so doing transforms its capacity to create and to respond to beauty. The golden moment of this particular revolutionary epic was Article 58. Colonel Shwartzman treasured it with a special affection. Since the Lubyanka possessed no heart whatsoever, the secret police responded with an alternate human faculty, the imagination. There was ample room for this, since like all great literary works, the Criminal Code of 1926 permitted various readings. No other article so captured his NKVD fantasy, challenging him to invent, to devise, to contrive, and to fabricate.

Article 58 recalled happier, more hopeful days, but Colonel Shwartzman's feelings went beyond sentiment. In great art a man can discover himself; he can develop in response to its liberating vision. Article 58 was his teacher; Article 58 had made him the fine Chekist that he was. With appreciation and devotion, the colonel performed as one of its finest explicators. So with an understandable pride, he warmed to the task. His exhilaration was suffused with a calm that came from confidence and from the very nature of the art form itself, which demanded precision and control. To the untrained eye, Article 58 with its fourteen sections seemed a drab, restricted piece of the Criminal Code concerned with crimes against the state. To the initiated, however, Article 58 was a sonnet awaiting the muses to grace its fourteen sections, wherein could be discovered the line, stanza, rhythm, and rhyme of counterrevolution.

Colonel Shwartzman turned to Section 1, on actions that weaken the power of the state. At once Grisha—for Grisha was the more artistic side of Colonel Shwartzman— saw the obvious interpretation of the prisoner's actions. Hadn't he raped the general secretary? Ah, but Stalin, it might be argued, had been smiling. That could be explained or even deleted, but the colonel (Grisha) was an artist; he sought the particular that illuminates.

"Dmitri, you have given us the broad outlines of your activities, but we will need details." He tapped his pistol. "When you were with the general secretary, did you in any way harm him? It might even have been a gesture or a look."

"Yes, I did, Citizen Colonel. Yes, I did," the prisoner said in quick repetition.

"Good, let's hear about it."

"It was an awful thing." The prisoner looked away. His eyes found the pistol and remained fixed upon its sheltering metal gleam, but his lips moved and his voice throbbed with his mortifying, stimulating story. "It will shock you, as well it should; night after night, it shocked me. In the moment of my greatest excitement, I lost all self-control, and I would reach down and squeeze Stalin's balls . . . and as I squeezed, he pissed blood."

The prisoner dropped his head in shame, but Colonel Shwartzman could barely keep from clapping his hands in joy. This was perfect. Under the recent revisions of 1934, Section 1b declared that any damage to the motherland's might was punishable by death. The sonnet was a subtle, complex form: the general secretary's inferior position suggested the motherland, but his balls and blood were pure masculine power.

It was even better than he had supposed at first glance: the colonel had worried that Section 2, armed rebellion, might elude him. Now it was inspired, the way everything was coming together. Section 2 defined armed rebellion as "seizure of power" and "dismembering any part of the USSR." What greater seizure of power could there be than

seizing Stalin's balls? What greater dismemberment of Russia than dismembering the Defender of the Peoples himself?
Thank heavens, Stalin had two balls—the traitor Trotsky
was rumored to have only one!—the prisoner would be
indicted (and confess, of course) under Section 1b for the
right ball, since that carried the death sentence, and under
Section 2 for the left. As for the actual dismemberment,
that was no problem, for Article 58 was part of a greater
work and was enriched by the entire opus. Article 19 explicitly stated that intent was sufficient grounds for convic-
tion; indeed there was no difference between intent and
commission of the crime itself. In any event, Stalin's piss-
ing blood could be interpreted as dismembering part of
Russia. What could be a more essential part of Russia than
the Beloved Leader's lifeblood?

Section 3 would have daunted lesser talents. Since the
USSR was not in a declared state of war, it was difficult to
imagine in what way the prisoner aided or abetted by any
means whatsoever the foreign enemy state. Article 58, however, was itself a gift of the imagination and inspired the
daring. The colonel had fought in the Civil War against
the forces of Britain, France, the United States, and other
minions of world capitalism. The noble Red Army had
driven them out of the motherland, but they had never
surrendered. If the world's only socialist republic were not
at war with world capitalism, then the word *war* had no
meaning. As for the prisoner's assistance to a foreign power,
that was clear. He had confessed to knowing Polish, English,
French, and German and was in charge of foreign collections at the library.

"Dmitri, do you encourage people to read your books?"

"Oh, yes, I love the books. They were my life until—"

"And many of these—say the English ones, for example, were printed in New York or London?"

"Yes."

"And the French in Paris."

"Yes."

"And you guided people to them and encouraged Soviet citizens to read them?"

"Yes."

"And soldiers, too?" the colonel asked.

"I don't exactly remember, but I must have," Dmitri answered.

"Among all the people you helped in the great Lenin Library, don't you think there were members of the glorious Red Army among them?" the colonel asked incredulously.

"If you put it that way, I am sure there certainly must have been," the prisoner agreed.

"I should hope so," the colonel concurred as he wrote, "Disseminating the vile propaganda of foreign powers at war with the beloved motherland among loyal members of the glorious Red Army."

He had considered asking the prisoner to confirm his contacts with foreign operatives, but artistic sense weighed against it. Any mention of foreign embassies and their operatives would confuse the weak-minded as to the existing state of war.

Section 4, succor to the international bourgeoisie, posed no problem. In this case, Section 3 could be interpreted as including Section 4—and its incumbent punishment, of course. To do that, however, would be cutting corners, and in a work of art one did not cut corners; one embellished them.

ALLEN HOFFMAN

"Dmitri, as an intellectual you must have friends like yourself," the Colonel suggested.

"I never had as many friends as I would have liked," the prisoner responded.

"Few of us do, but among the intellectuals there was always a heavy representation of Mensheviks. There aren't so many Mensheviks as there used to be, but I'm sure you remember some," he coaxed.

"Mensheviks? At first everyone was a Bolshevik or Menshevik, weren't they?" Dmitri asked.

"You see, you must have known them well!"

"I suppose so. My landlord was one, I think, but he's a very good citizen," Dmitri stressed.

"Everyone thought you were a good citizen, too, didn't they?" the colonel reminded him.

The prisoner nodded.

"It is only for the state security to decide who is a good citizen. Only we know."

Again Dmitri Cherbyshev nodded.

"Good, what is his name? It's a mere formality," the colonel added.

"Ivan Molchanov," the prisoner said hesitantly.

"Does the name Sergei Gasparov mean anything to you?"

"No, I don't think so. Should it?" the prisoner inquired apologetically.

"I just thought it might. You might have heard it and don't remember it," the interrogator suggested casually.

"That could be. I'm not very good at people's names unless they have written books."

"I should hope so," the colonel agreed, entering "Co-conspirators Ivan Molchanov and Sergei Gasparov, agents of the international Menshevik bourgeoisie," in the file.

As he wrote the name of his antagonist of the morning, he felt the warm satisfaction of tying loose ends together. True Chekist economy! It was just as well that he had been so lenient in not sending Gasparov to a punishment cell.

Colonel Shwartzman's spirits flagged slightly as he approached Section 5, "Inciting a foreign state to declare war against the USSR." Then suddenly he saw it! Just because the foreign capitalist states were at war with the USSR in Section 3 didn't mean that they had declared war. If they had, then Section 5, the declaring of war, should have preceded Section 3. And it most certainly did not. Why not? Because of cases like this, when the USSR was involved in an undeclared war and an anti-Soviet agent like Dmitri Cherbyshev was working to invite a declaration of war in order to mobilize additional imperialist powers to fight against the USSR.

"No doubt some of the embassies here in Moscow must have sent their personnel to use the foreign collections in the library," the colonel suggested.

"Occasionally they required books. I would send the volumes to the director's office," Dmitri answered.

"The director's name?"

"Yuri Yasni."

The colonel was pleased to involve the Lenin Library's director. Different defendants for each section added a richness and breadth to the confession, not to mention the more obvious virtue of suggesting that the central defendant was a very big fish indeed.

Section 6, espionage, presented the colonel with a delicate problem. Since everyone in Moscow was a spy—with the aid of Article 19, intent equals the crime itself—this was usually the easiest of charges. But what was Dmitri's spying? Stalin's backside! Indelicate in the extreme. Spies invariably had contacts and accomplices. Here lay the great fear: might Stalin not be a suspect? Or at the very least a dupe? Nonsense! No one could suggest that the Genius of Humanity lacked revolutionary vigilance. He had purged the party and its leaders, finding spies, saboteurs, and wreckers everywhere. How could Dmitri Cherbyshev have snuck up his unsuspecting asshole? The colonel sat and pondered, and he was rewarded for his efforts. Under Section 6 one could be convicted just as easily for suspicion of espionage or contacts leading to suspicion of espionage. The colonel leaned toward the latter charge. For such a crime, the accused might be shot, but it left the target of his seduction several steps removed.

Finally, under contacts leading to suspicion of espionage, the colonel accused the prisoner of "clumsy attempts to penetrate the Soviet body politic from the rear."

Wrecking in the classic sense was the subject of Section 7, "Subverting various elements of the economy such as industry, agriculture, transport, or the circulation of money." The colonel hesitated; after all, he was dealing with the general secretary, even if indirectly.

"Dmitri, did you at any time offer the general secretary money?" the interrogator asked gingerly. He was afraid that the prisoner might answer that Stalin had offered him rubles. Then he would have a problem on his hands.

"No, I thought that in our society, we have very little

need for money," Dmitri answered, slightly bewildered. "I never asked, but I imagine he gets a respectable salary."

"I'm sure he does, but I was inquiring into your relationship with the general secretary for the purposes of our report. In your extended and frequent encounters, did anything of value ever exchange hands?"

The prisoner sat up; his large, tired eyes kindled with the inward glow of memory.

"Yes, once. Only once. I remember," he announced, very pleased with himself.

"Good. Let's hear about it."

"I don't exactly remember why, but once he turned around and pinned a medal on my dick. A Hero of Red Labor." The prisoner came as close to a smile as he had all day.

"What did you do with this valuable decoration?"

"Well, that's just the thing. It was very uncomfortable. I just couldn't get the thing off. It became a terrible nuisance. Finally, I couldn't hold it in any longer. When I urinated, the metal rusted. The ribbon dried quickly enough, but the metal was completely destroyed. It rusted through and dropped off. You can imagine my relief when it did. I had already ruined my underwear. Even now—"

The colonel interrupted him. "Thank you, I think we have what we want," he said, as he indicted the prisoner for "a thorough and protracted attempt to corrode the value of socialist labor and socialist institutions."

When he arrived at Section 8, "Terror—including threats and attacks on party members," the colonel decided to delete Stalin's blood from Section 2 ("Severing any part of the USSR") and identify the blood that the prisoner had squeezed from Stalin as the proof of a terrorist attack. He was pleased with the symmetry of the solution. Sections 1 and 2 referred to the state itself. Allotting the general secretary's testicles, one each, to these sections had a pleasing parallelism, whereas the spilled blood provided a precise image of terrorist attack against a defenseless innocent.

Before he could fully relish the elegantly balanced poetries of terror, he faced the challenge of Section 9's merciless specificity, "Destruction or damage by explosion or arson." The colonel simply had no ideas. He fell back on the interrogator's last resort: fishing.

"Do you recall any flames or fires during your sessions with the general secretary?"

"No," the prisoner answered.

"Sparks?"

"No."

"Anything that looked like a fire?" he suggested.

"No."

"Maybe someone was flushed and ran a slight fever?" the colonel implored.

"I'm sorry," the prisoner answered in disappointment.

"Yes, so am I," agreed the colonel.

Dejected, they sat staring at one another.

"What about an explosion?" the colonel suggested in desperation.

"Explosion?" the prisoner repeated, as if it were the strangest word imaginable.

"Yes, was there anything that seemed like an explosion?"

The prisoner considered the question. "Just what I told you about earlier."

"What was that?" the colonel wondered.

"In the moment of my greatest excitement, I lost control of myself, and that was when I squeezed the general secretary's balls and he pissed blood," the prisoner repeated.

The colonel sat up.

"You mean that was an explosive moment?" he asked enthusiastically.

"Yes, when I was most excited. You know how it is. It's like you're exploding," he said delicately.

"You mean exploding like *that?*" the colonel confirmed.

"Yes," the prisoner whispered.

"Wonderful," the colonel rejoiced. "And this happened on more than one occasion?"

"Every night for two years!"

"Fine," the colonel nodded and wrote, "Purposely polluted essential party processes through explosive acts."

Section 9 had turned out surprisingly well. The colonel had always been sure of Section 10. He had seen its development from the very beginning. Under Section 10, any propaganda or agitation that appealed for the overthrow or weakening of the Soviet government was declared illegal. Such agitation might be oral or written. The prisoner had written to the NKVD that he wanted to confess. The NKVD received a great many letters of revelation, but the authors invariably revealed someone else's wrongdoing. A missive begging to confess was a rare communication. Clearly this unusual letter—even the bizarre confession itself—contained an appeal to weaken Soviet power. Colonel Shwartzman made a note that the prisoner's correspondence with the NKVD should be entered under Section 10. Documentary evidence, especially if written by the defendant himself, added a certain completeness to the indictment.

Section 10 was a good piece of work, but it lacked the sense of discovery and spontaneity that informed some of his other masterstrokes. He was philosophical: that was part of the creative process; it couldn't be all unalloyed joy.

The general secretary proved a complicating or an "aggravating" factor in Section 11, which declared that if any actions covered by the preceding actions had been the act of an organization, then they were to be viewed much more severely. As a general rule, any and all sexual activity fell under Section 11. After all, it takes two to tango. In this particular dance, however, the partner was Iosif Vissarionovich Stalin. How could the prisoner have been a member of the organization and Stalin not? From the prisoner's point of view, Stalin was a willing participant and, consequently, a member of the organization. Of course, such an idea was impossible! Adopting a literal interpretation of the events, the colonel therefore cited the general secretary for "his revealing participation as an undercover agent of the toiling Soviet masses."

Colonel Shwartzman finished Section 11 and turned to the prisoner.

"Dmitri, in your letter to the NKVD, did you tell them the nature of your activities?"

"No, I just said that I wanted to confess some very inappropriate behavior," the prisoner admitted.

The colonel turned back to his report, condemning Dmitri Cherbyshev both for "failing to denounce" the director of the Lenin Library for passing Soviet property to foreigners and for failing to detail his own crimes in his letter to the NKVD.

"Dmitri, in your professional capacity at the library, do

you remember handling any books about the tsarist secret police, the Okhrana?" the colonel asked gravely.

"I'm not sure," the prisoner mumbled.

"It's very important that if you did, you did so as an employee of the Lenin Library," the colonel insisted.

"In the foreign sections, we have some material, but—"

"No," the colonel interrupted. "We want Russian books printed before the revolution that have sections discussing the tsarist secret police."

Deeply desirous of pleasing, the prisoner sat thinking, then looked up eagerly.

"In the reference room I remember handing people some of the old almanacs. They were printed before October 1917, and they certainly have passages describing all branches of the tsarist government."

"You're certain about that?" the colonel asked skeptically.

"Absolutely, Citizen Colonel."

"And you knew that such material was in those books when you handed them to the readers?"

"Yes, I must have. Any librarian would," the prisoner declared.

"Good. We have made progress," the colonel announced.

The anxious prisoner seemed pleased, and so did his NKVD investigator, who accused him under Section 13 of serving in the dreaded Okhrana, the tsarist secret police. Understandably, this was a broad interpretation of the section, but the colonel felt entitled to some poetic license as he penned the penultimate stanza of his sonnet.

Approaching the final section, 14, the colonel had a sense of achievement, but he wanted to finish with a bang, something really special. On a mundane level, this section talked about "not fulfilling one's economic obligations," but "economic sabotage" also had its broader context. And that was where artistry lay.

"Dmitri, you have spoken about the blood you squeezed out of the general secretary. Aside from that abnormal emission, were there more normal ones?" he asked delicately.

"You mean like . . . you would expect?" the prisoner responded with equal delicacy.

"Uh-huh," the colonel replied.

"Yes, there were."

"There were?"

"Many more than you would expect. He's a very great man," the prisoner said reverently.

"Uh-huh." The colonel coughed in embarrassment and described in detail under Section 14 how Dmitri Cherbyshev destroyed the most precious potential of the Russian people and the world's masses by wasting the Great Genius's seed.

CHAPTER FIVE

WITH A SENSE OF SATISFACTION BORDERING ON DELIGHT, the colonel finished the statement and brought it around to the prisoner.

"You sign right here," he ordered.

The prisoner dutifully took the pen. Although careful not to reveal any emotion, the colonel waited with mounting excitement for the condemned prisoner to scratch his name on the bottom of the final page. Instead, the prisoner signed with ease and fluency. Grisha hadn't believed the man capable of such a sustained rapid action. The strong, graceful signature suggested the art of calligraphy. This unexpected artistry impressed the investigator; Dmitri Cherbyshev's signature was fully worthy of the brilliant poem the colonel had crafted from Article 58. It was as if the prisoner understood and complemented the colonel's own performance. No longer feeling quite so alone, Grisha Shwartzman had a sudden impulse to continue his conversation with Dmitri Cherbyshev. He returned to Svetkov's impressive chair and sat down, all the while savoring their joint creation.

"Dmitri, I'm very proud of you," the colonel said. He refrained from adding that he wished that he himself had such a beautiful signature. He would have to take extra care to sign his own name with all the precision of line he could muster so as not to disgrace their mutual effort.

The colonel's compliment confused the prisoner. He stared intently with his fearful, questioning eyes at the investigator. Was the colonel indulging in sarcasm?

"We have here a very fine piece of work, one that we can both be proud of. Your signature is a work of art, worthy of Article 58. I am embarrassed to sign beneath you," Grisha explained.

Dmitri Cherbyshev nodded, still perplexed.

"Very lovely signature," Grisha repeated.

"I was criticized for it at the library," Dmitri said.

"Really?"

"They told me it was not proletarian. They said I suffered from bourgeois pretensions," Dmitri explained in a flat, exhausted tone, as if he accepted the truth of those charges.

"Do you think they're right?" Grisha asked.

Although Grisha wanted to talk with him, Dmitri Cherbyshev remained the Lubyanka prisoner and merely shrugged, suggesting that such matters were not for him to decide.

"What do *you* think, Dmitri?" Grisha asked.

Dmitri squirmed uncomfortably. "I don't know. I suppose so. After all this business, I just don't know. They warned me about the other, and they were right about that, weren't they? Day after day."

Grisha's attempt at dialogue was not progressing very far, but he didn't want Dmitri to leave. Where could Grisha go, and what could he do? For all the beauty and originality of the confession, both Grisha and Hershel Shwartzman sensed on some level that they had fallen into a trap. Yes, it was an imaginative realization of Article 58, but it contained one tragic flaw: blasphemy, an unflattering portrayal of the general secretary, the Great Genius, Iosif Vissarionovich himself. Yes, the colonel should have shot this disgusting filth of a prisoner between those wide eyes and informed the efficient Tatiana that a counterrevolutionary stain spotted the Lubyanka carpet. She would have known what to do, and the carpet would have been cleaner than before. Colonel Shwartzman could have returned his softly smoking pistol to its holster, where its gentle explosive warmth could burrow through the leather and cloth to nestle on his thigh. But he had not done so, and with nowhere to go and nothing to do, Grisha and the colonel felt the return of the unrelenting itch of prurient curiosity that they had stifled earlier.

"Every day for two years?" Grisha resumed.

"Yes," the prisoner admitted shamefully.

"But you must have enjoyed it?" Grisha suggested.

The prisoner stared at Grisha in discomfort. He began to speak, but no sound emerged from his agonized lips.

"You didn't enjoy it?"

With more control over his lips—and less over his eyes, which tilted upward in distress—Dmitri managed to speak. "Disgusting. Something so shameful. How could I?" His voice was surprisingly strong.

"You did it every night," Grisha insisted.

Dmitri Cherbyshev didn't deny it.

"Was anyone forcing you to do it?"

"Forcing me?" the prisoner repeated.

"Yes, was anyone forcing you?"

Dmitri seemed unsure. "Who?"

Grisha took another tack. "Did Stalin enjoy it?"

Embarrassment flushed across his face. He nodded.

"Are you sure?" Grisha quizzed.

Again Dmitri nodded.

"You're so unsure of everything. How can you be so sure of this?"

"I'm sure," Dmitri insisted with quiet certainty.

"Dmitri, we're here to tell the truth, aren't we?"

Dmitri nodded.

"Then tell me what happened," the colonel ordered.

"How can I lie? Stalin smiles when I explode in him." Dmitri responded to the order quietly but naturally, revealing little of his usual shame.

"But if you were on top, how could you tell he was smiling?"

"He would twist his head around and grin, with that broad mustache and those lynxlike Georgian eyes, like a cat. A selfish, spiteful cat, whose good time was always at someone else's expense." Dmitri related all this quietly, but a bitterness had crept into his voice at the mention of the Georgian cat.

"Surely he wasn't so cruel. He did let you get on top," Grisha said, defending the general secretary.

"He was full of tricks. Why do you think he smiled?" Dmitri asked sardonically.

"I suppose he was enjoying himself."

"Of course, but not the way you think," Dmitri replied bitterly.

"No?"

"No. When he turned around, he was drawing away from me. He liked it all right, but that was why he smiled, to torture me further!"

"Perhaps he wasn't aware of the discomfort he was causing you? Did you ever discuss it with him?"

"Who can talk to a cat? He knew what he was doing, and so did I," the prisoner answered.

"You did?"

"He got me excited, and then, pretending to show me his enjoyment, he tried to crawl away. But I didn't let him. I stayed right behind him, crashing into him all the time. Sometimes I bumped him so hard his hat came off. You know, the one with the little beak and red star. More often than not, we would swarm right over it as I kept on top of him."

The colonel made a mental note to add the crushed hat to Section 9, "Destruction through explosion," and to Section 14, "Economic sabotage." He wondered whether he could acquire a similar hat for evidence.

"He controlled everything. Stalin wanted to cheat me, too," Dmitri said sourly. "Still, he was the general secretary. At the most passionate moments, a part of me felt a cold shame. I would think, 'How can I be doing this to Mother Russia?'"

Dmitri paused reflectively, as if recapturing the tension of the moment. Respectful, Grisha did not interrupt.

"And even that was another of Stalin's lies. I wasn't anywhere near Mother Russia. When I arrived, do you know what I found? Georgian shit! Spicy, greasy shishlik on my skewer. It wasn't Russian at all. Stalin's asshole was filled with *kharcho,* you know, that spicy, greasy soup. Those awful *tchboureki.* Have you ever had that dough with the meat and onions boiled in oil?"

Dmitri looked inquisitively at his NKVD interrogator. Grisha merely shook his head.

"You aren't missing anything. Night after night, I would refuse to touch it, and Stalin would lick it off with relish. He's really a very simple soul; that part is true. Not at all a snob; I'll say that for him. Very down to earth. But I hated it."

"Yes, but you did it," Grisha countered.

"In Russia, what does that prove? Only that I had to. Do you think anyone in Russia does anything for any reason other than that he has to?"

Grisha didn't respond.

"None of that Kirov murder business makes any sense, except for one thing. You can be sure of this: if Leonid Niko-layev shot Kirov, he did so because he had to," Dmitri stated.

"The state security services have proved that other counterrevolutionary groups were involved," Grisha said, challenging the hypothesis.

"That may be so. I don't know, but in that case, then not only the assassin had to do it. Others, too."

The prisoner's insistence, although powerful, was not offensively dogmatic. After the bitterness, Dmitri Cherby-shev had arrived at hopeless resignation.

"I'm not sure I understand," Grisha said.

"Yes, unfortunately, you do," the prisoner stated with a deep sadness.

"I do?" Grisha asked curiously.

"Yes," the prisoner reiterated.

"What makes you so sure?" the NKVD officer asked in slight annoyance.

Dmitri squirmed uncomfortably.

"For a moment, I thought you would shoot me, but you understood me, so you couldn't. A man in your position isn't afraid to pull a trigger. You didn't shoot me because you couldn't."

"You don't think I can do it now if I want to?" Grisha challenged.

The prisoner shook his head. Grisha picked up the pistol and pointed it at Dmitri, who regarded it with wide-eyed boredom. Grisha lowered the pistol and slipped it back into his holster. Even through the leather, he felt its cool, inert metallic bulk.

"Why not? Why can't I?"

"Stalin controls you, too. He controls everything."

"You know, I really should have shot you. You know that, don't you?" Grisha asked irrelevantly.

"Yes, but you couldn't. That's why they brought me to you."

Grisha wasn't so sure that Dmitri Cherbyshev was wrong.

"Who is 'they'?" he inquired lamely.

"You know better than I do. The important thing is that *they* knew you would understand, and they were right," Dmitri explained.

Grisha sat silently. Was "they" Svetkov? Was "they" Yezhov, head of the NKVD? Or was "they" Stalin himself? Did it matter? They knew, all right.

"May I ask you a question?" Dmitri asked. Momentarily he looked away. When he turned back, his face flushed slightly with embarrassment and curiosity.

Grisha was still mulling over the identity of "they." He didn't really know, and he didn't discourage Dmitri from asking him anything.

"You hate Trotsky with a vengeance. You must think about him often." Dmitri paused, inviting a response.

"Sometimes," Grisha confessed, although he wanted to remain noncommittal.

"Tell me," Dmitri Cherbyshev asked in a low, husky voice, "When you do it with Trotsky, are you on the top or the bottom?"

"What?!" Grisha choked in shocked astonishment. "What are you saying?"

Dmitri Cherbyshev didn't turn away, but his face flushed red. "Forgive my asking," he stammered.

"Are you crazy?" Grisha hurled at him.

Dmitri looked down at his feet. When he heard no further invective, he looked up to discover the NKVD colonel pointing his pistol directly at him. Dmitri seemed confused and no longer eager for the NKVD man to pull the trigger.

Outraged, Grisha held the gun for half a minute and then with his free hand reached for the telephone.

"Return the prisoner to his cell immediately," he commanded and hung up.

He lowered his pistol and placed it on the desk. Still furious, but confused—this was a different carousel, but moving every bit as fast—he continued to stare at the prisoner.

"Thank you," Dmitri whispered.

"I thought you wanted to die," Grisha said.

"I do, but because of Stalin, not because of you—or Trotsky or anyone else," the prisoner answered softly.

Grisha didn't have to respond, for the guard knocked on the door. Grisha ordered the prisoner to be returned to his cell until further notice. Dmitri Cherbyshev rose and left the room as he had entered, under guard and with the wide-eyed, fearful, slow grace of the night-shadowed jungle. But this time no one mistook him for Leon Trotsky. Least of all Grisha, who studiously observed the departure. Then he methodically returned his pistol to its blocky holster.

He reached for the phone and ordered a car to take him home. As he rose from the chief investigator's desk, he folded the several pages of the confession and put them in his tunic pocket. He could no longer smooth the garment, for the report filled the square pocket and formed a low, flat bulge like a brick.

When he passed by Tatiana, he said nothing. In fact, he hardly noticed her. He just wanted to get out of the dark jungle of the Lubyanka.

He had wanted to shoot, but how could he? He feared that if he squeezed the trigger, blood would spurt forth in a dark staining stream.

CHAPTER SIX

SIGNING OUT OF THE PRISON, GRISHA WAS SEIZED BY fear. He glanced at the large clock on the wall above the duty ledger to discover that it was already 3:00 P.M. Much later than he had thought, but he was so distraught that the hour made little impression on him. He had no sensation of hunger, although he had not eaten since the night before. But even though he gazed wearily at the clock, he did not feel tired. He stared too long. As the desktop had fascinated him earlier, so the timepiece did now. The clock face with its routine, placid symmetry mirrored his own outward calm; behind the simple exterior, however, an unsightly frenzied mass of gears, flywheels, and springs gnashed, pressed, spun, and ground against one another— brutal, abrasive, and degenerative.

All of this mechanical turbulence leached forth at an imperceptible rate. Grisha examined the second hand but could not detect any movement. He fixed his gaze even more resolutely, but the motion eluded him. He knew that it had to be moving. Where were the simple hands going?

Rotating upon themselves in circles like a carousel; but unlike the carousel, their revolutions were mercifully slow. Grisha wanted to leave, but he was afraid of what he would find in the Lubyanka's interior court.

"Colonel, your car is ready," the duty officer announced.

The man's voice was calm and matter-of-fact. The plot need not include him. Still, "they" would want to be certain, and the more mesh in the net, the more certainty of catching the fish. Grisha nodded and took a final glance at the clock. 3:02 P.M. He walked down the hallway, and the guard opened the door. Hit by a wave of bright natural light, Grisha blinked, but he could see another open door, that of a sedan. Once inside the car, he would be trapped. Colonel Shwartzman, with the brusque air of command, hurried out of the building and clambered into the car.

"Let's go!" he said imperiously to the uniformed driver, who held the door open for him.

"Yes, sir," the NKVD corporal responded quickly, slamming the rear door before opening the front one and seating himself behind the wheel.

The familiar car had often been at his disposal: a black Italian Fiat several years old, but still serviceable. In contrast, the driver was completely new. As Grisha stepped toward the automobile, he had managed a quick glance out of the corner of his eye. Standing stiffly erect, a stranger held the door. Grisha had seen other "new guards" like him. Too young to have experienced the revolution, they lacked imagination and individual personalities. Fervent in serving Stalin but without any passion for ideology or society, impersonal, almost mechanical, they were well trained and thoroughly reliable. And very well groomed, too. This had initially impressed Grisha and made him hopeful for his own future in the organization, but his burst of hope had been short-lived. Even their precisely uniformed and neat appearance marked them as "new men." Old Chekists cut a neat figure in their uniforms, but in a gallant, personal manner—as with Grisha's reflexive habit of smoothing his tunic to his body. With Stalin's new men, it was the other way round; they seemed to be smoothing their flesh to the uniforms. Passionless, nameless, they followed brutal orders, never bothering to justify themselves. The uniform was the sole license they required. Grisha hated the buffoonish Svetkov, but at least he knew who Svetkov was. Who were these "new men"? Who were "they"?

"You're new," Grisha commented.

"Corporal Orlov at your service, Citizen Colonel," the driver answered in forceful introduction.

Grisha was continually astonished at their effrontery. These days a raw corporal in the Lubyanka deigned to greet a full colonel. Under the corporal's hat, his black hair shaded to an even, bristly line before fading on the nape of his neck. Grisha wondered whether there was an NKVD barber he didn't know about who performed this tonsorial splendor on the new men. It was very impressive. Grisha's own hair had always been slightly ratty in back. What about Svetkov's? He couldn't remember. Svetkov was a mess; how long could he last with these automatons? In their heartless efficiency, they would tear him into neat little pieces—if Svetkov could be made neat, they were his only chance! It was almost enough to make Grisha feel sorry for his buffoonish superior.

Corporal Orlov started the motor, which responded

with a counterrevolutionary sputter before faltering altogether. After two more anti-Soviet misfires, the obstruc-
tionist engine turned over and succumbed to the organs'
demands. The old Fiat was fortunate that it was merely a
machine. Foreign Communists who proved more amenable
to serving Stalin had already been liquidated. The old,
worn black car was familiar; the driver was not. Again,
Grisha had to give the devil his due; the new man was in
better shape than the old automobile.

Corporal Orlov deftly put the automobile into gear, and
they began to emerge from the dirty, cavernous prison walls.
They crawled across the cobblestones toward the arch
where the great steel barricade separated the Lubyanka
from the streets of Moscow. The formidable gate swung
open, and the shadow-black automobile slid through the
fortress walls.

Grisha's sense of relief was minimal as they rolled alongside the NKVD headquarters.

"How do you know where I am going?" he asked in a
gentle, patronizing voice, amazed at the driver's temerity;
he hadn't asked his destination nor, at the very least, confirmed it.

"Your secretary said to take you to your home, Citizen
Colonel," the driver answered succinctly, with no hint of
apology. If anything, rather the opposite.

"You know where that is?" the colonel asked.

"We have been thoroughly briefed," the driver assured
him with the condescending efficiency that made Grisha
feel very old, almost a relic. He glanced at the familiar walls
of the ancient Lubyanka. Compared to the harsh, impersonal, impudent exterior of the back of the driver's head,

the modeled neo-Renaissance facade with its short, fluted columns and soaring sculpted ones topped by protruding capitals, balustrades, and pedimented windows seemed soft and almost personal.

Orlov's dark expanse of hair over his narrow strip of pale neck was a perverse anthropomorphic inversion of the Lubyanka, Grisha reflected, with the dark, rough-cut orthogonal stones at the base and the lighter Renaissance decorations above. Since Grisha was between the back of the driver's head and the wall of the Lubyanka, it seemed to him that the image was inverted as it passed through him. He found the corporal's neatly barbered scalp much more repulsive. Grisha imagined the back of Maya Kirsanova's head, with the delicious long blond hairs straying with sensual allure down over her supple neck, his tongue chasing them in sudden pursuit. Before he captured them, images inverted again, and he saw Dmitri Cherbyshev upside down, timidly crawling down the wall of the Lubyanka. Grisha rubbed his eyes.

"Where do you get your hair cut?" Grisha asked.

"What?" Corporal Orlov stammered. The unexpected question had caught him off guard.

"Your hair. Where did you get it cut?" Grisha repeated, as if it were the most routine question an NKVD colonel might ask.

"At home," the driver answered without any of his cockiness. Slightly embarrassed, he flushed pink on his bare neck. Grisha thought he saw him squirm uncomfortably. He imagined the man to be gripping the wheel. Apparently he hadn't been trained to answer this particular question.

"At home," Grisha repeated, to prolong the man's discomfort.

"My wife does it," the driver explained apologetically.

Grisha had not imagined Corporal Orlov as married. The new breed seemed so passionless and so dedicated, almost wedded to Stalin. What kind of marriage could they have? Whose hand ran the sharp scissors over his head? Might even Tatiana the mule be married? The thought that such sterile people should successfully marry distressed him. Perhaps they merely shared apartments, and when they found themselves in the same room, they silently cut each other's hair. Their hair seemed to be growing shorter and shorter.

"Does your wife work for us, too?" Grisha inquired.

"No, she is at the Bureau of Electricity."

"Very important, electricity," Grisha mused.

Corporal Orlov nodded.

"Do you cut her hair?" Grisha asked.

The driver was surprised by the question. "No, her friend does it."

"I see," Grisha said, but he really didn't. Not the corporal's wife's haircut, anyway. What he did see was the elevated embankment of the Karl Marx Prospekt sliding by on his left. Somewhere behind him would be the statue of Ivan Fyodorov, who printed the first Russian book. But that had been years ago, under the stars. How many? Three, four, five hundred years ago? Grisha made a mental note that he should check the date on the base of the statue. Did it have a date? He didn't know. He gradually became aware that the driver was saying something. Corporal Orlov no longer seemed quite so self-conscious.

Grisha commanded his subordinate to repeat his words.

"I said Colonel Svetkov told me to deliver a package to you, sir. He said it's a gift," the driver repeated bloodlessly.

"What package?"

"The one next to you," the driver answered.

Looking down on the seat next to him, Grisha discovered an unobtrusive cloth shopping bag that was almost the same color as the dark faded leather of the old Fiat upholstery.

"From Svetkov?" he asked.

"Yes, from the colonel," the driver replied.

Grisha lifted the soft cloth bag. He felt something hard and cylindrical inside. Later, he thought that he should have guessed what the buffoonish Svetkov had deposited in his lap, but initially he had no idea. He innocently opened the floppy cloth mouth to discover the bottle of kosher wine. Although the bottle lacked any label and was refitted with an old cap, Grisha had no doubt as to its contents. Filled almost to the top of its thin, protrusive neck, it seemed to come to life in his hand, trilling its bubble-filled air space back and forth in response to the Fiat's encounter with Karl Marx Prospekt. When the aerated bubbles leaped toward him, he could detect a faint purplish tint that quickly descended into the brackish darkness of the bag. He closed the bag and calmly placed it on the seat next to him, as if he had picked it up by mistake.

Grisha sensed that his life depended on ignoring the nondescript object that he had stumbled across, the way a resting woodsman realizes that he is sharing his log with a poisonous serpent. He felt as if he were cradling blood on his lap. Had he already been bitten? He forced himself to remain calm, but he could feel his temples pulsing, and he had a nearly overwhelming desire to scream. A constricted feeling gripped him, as if he were imprisoned in the automobile. Feverishly, he stared at the world outside.

The old official Fiat seemed to be crawling along the bottom of some deep ocean canyon. The soaring neoclassical columns of the Bolshoi Theater dwarfed the other buildings and accentuated Grisha's insignificance, as if he were a captive of a small black Fiat bug that had crawled out of the dark nest of the Lubyanka. Where was it taking him?

The black bug dragged Grisha through the bright sterile void toward a narrow slit where Karl Marx Prospekt squeezed itself between the old Grand Hotel and the Trade Union House. Grisha recoiled as if his heart were contracting in mortal fear. The small, stately Trade Union House on his right flashed the image of death. Once a nobleman's club, it had retained its noble purpose if not its class orientation. Grisha had heard Lenin speak there, and twelve years earlier he had filed past when the Father of Revolution lay in state. Amidst the jumble of funereal memories, perhaps stimulated by them, Grisha imagined that he was being driven to his own "final resting place." Lenin lying waxen on his trade union bier suddenly appeared as a very frightening precursor of Grisha's fate.

He knew—you lost your grip, the carousel turned; dizzy, you flew toward the crash from which you never arose. He shuddered at the still corpse of Lenin. Lenin, who had so much energy; Lenin, who possessed so much life—Lenin, whose little finger could command the attention of millions—lay so grotesquely still. Grisha shuddered, but even in his fear he experienced a sense of relief as they approached the broad open expanse of Manege Square. His dark insect captor paused at the intersection of Karl Marx Prospekt and Gorky Street to permit a bus that was pulling away from the Moscow Hotel to cross.

But as the intersection cleared, Grisha knew his reprieve to be temporary. After several moments upon the open floor of Manege Square, the automated insect—human compared to its mechanized driver—would drag Grisha off into the narrow, suffocating lanes of the Arbat district. Where would it deposit him? The bug couldn't possibly take him home. Not to his home, anyway. The NKVD drone might very well drag him back to an NKVD cranny—if not the mother hive of the Lubyanka—and there sting Grisha to death so the whole colony could feed off him, or more accurately, off his murder; from some the NKVD wanted their bodies, from others their blood, and from yet others, both. Since they—who were "they"?—wanted his blood, his category seemed the worst of all.

"Stop!" Colonel Hershel Shwartzman commanded with crisp, almost fierce authority.

The car slowed.

"Right here!" the colonel demanded in a tone that didn't permit argument.

Corporal Orlov stopped the automobile and turned toward his passenger for an explanation. Instead, brown shopping bag in hand, Grisha leaped out of the limousine into the street. Before the driver could inquire as to further instructions, his passenger was already crossing the sidewalk and striding briskly toward the entrance of the National Hotel.

Without looking back, Grisha entered the hotel. The

doorman deferentially greeted the NKVD colonel by quickly opening the door. Grisha entered the lobby and slowed down. He walked toward the desk, looked around the lobby as if futilely searching for someone, glanced impatiently at his watch. Then he turned to leave, waving away the clerk who was hurrying over to assist him.

"May I help you, Citizen Colonel?" the man called from a respectful distance.

"Have you seen Orlov?" Grisha demanded.

"I don't think I know Orlov," the man stammered.

"Then you certainly can't help me," Grisha answered as he turned toward the door.

"Does he work here?" the clerk asked fearfully.

Curious to see if Orlov had followed him into the hotel, Grisha continued toward the door. He left the National Hotel and was pleased to discover that Corporal Orlov and the black Fiat were nowhere in sight. Assuming that the corporal would not abandon the automobile unless he had some very specific mission, Grisha had fled with Svetkov's diabolical gift. Corporal Orlov would have pursued him on foot through all of Moscow to execute Svetkov's order, but now the driver would most probably return to the Lubyanka and report Grisha's escape. No doubt he had not been given instructions as to what he should do in such an eventuality. Why should he have? Where could Grisha go?

What did it matter? There was no escape. Whatever fate "they" had prepared for him this afternoon would still be there tomorrow. Grisha knew the game; he had played it often enough. A car pulls up to the curb, and two gentlemen politely invite the victim to come with them to clarify some routine matter. How can one refuse such a reasonable, insistent request? It won't take very long to clarify such a humdrum detail. It is even true: for the NKVD it is a routine matter. As for clarification, he is under arrest. What could be clearer? And it doesn't take long once he enters the car. Astonished, outraged, protesting his innocence—there must be some mistake—the victim refuses to accept the quick, painless clarity of Soviet justice.

Sergei Gasparov must have been like that; fuming with indignation and demanding to know on whose authority they were acting. Grisha enjoyed the idea of a bewildered Menshevik, but his pleasure was short-lived. No, the hard, fearless Gasparov was never bewildered. He must have made even his first investigating officer's life uncomfortable. He had certainly made Grisha uncomfortable. For that matter, so had Dmitri Cherbyshev, but Grisha felt a wave of revulsion at the thought of those unnaturally large, shame-filled eyes. He couldn't think about him. The misty eyes made him uneasy, and Dmitri Cherbyshev didn't really fit into either category—and that made Grisha even more uncomfortable. One thing that the NKVD offered was categories; Article 58 of the Criminal Code was a perfect example.

No, with Grisha they were playing the other game, cat and mouse. Grisha had executed it well himself when the occasion had called for it, but he had never really liked it. Grisha preferred a quick, clean arrest. No doubt Svetkov thrived on the other. Once you have someone in your clutches, you let him turn every which way but loose. Orlov the driver might be disciplined for losing his captive, but Svetkov wouldn't be upset. Svetkov's sewerlike mouth would fall open, and he would guffaw in arrogant conceit when he heard that Grisha had taken the cursed wine.

The chance that the NKVD driver might be circling the area in search of him inspired Grisha to start walking. He looked down the street toward the great columned exhibition hall, the Manege, where the tsar had once trained his horses, then he turned back to cross the exceptionally broad street where Karl Marx Prospekt met Manege Square. With the brown cloth bag clutched firmly under his arm—he could hear the miserable Jewish wine gurgling inside as if it were praying—he walked toward the Kremlin, as if drawn toward the heart of all Russia itself.

CHAPTER SEVEN

GRISHA TRUDGED ACROSS THE STARK OPEN SPACE, picking his way among the sparse vehicular traffic toward the rich, deep green of the splendid Alexandrovsky Gardens that nestled at the base of the Kremlin wall. The solid brick wall basked ancient in the September sun, glowing with an earthen redness that seemed, for all its solidity, softer and more personal than the heavy stone and cement masonry of the more modern city. Even if it now guarded the riddle of communism and protected Stalin himself, the Kremlin for centuries had hidden more arcane secrets, had protected more splendid tyrants, for so long and so well that it had become part of the enigma itself: no one entered then, no one entered now.

On occasion, armed with a special pass, feeling alien, Colonel Hershel Shwartzman had crossed its timeless threshold. Now he had no desire to do so. What business could he have with Stalin? The image of the mustachioed Genius of World Revolution danced somewhere in the Kremlin. With trembling fingers, Grisha felt the stiff folds of Dmitri

Cherbyshev's confession; the Kremlin's massive base, brick upon brick, seemed barely thick enough to blot out the cat-like grin. Beneath the arsenal tower, Grisha hurried into the surrounding garden and plunged into the cool emerald shade. Not wanting to linger by the entrance, he did not pause to acknowledge or to savor the vernal greeting, but continued down the walk.

At the first open space, where his attention was caught by the tall sentry of a monumental obelisk, he burst into laughter. Not a peal of mad hilarity, but an earnest laugh at the joke that stood so erectly before him, the Monument to Revolutionary Thinkers, whose names were incised into the stone—Marx, Engels, Liebknecht, Lasalle, Bebel, Campanella, Moore, Saint-Simon, Bakunin, and others. What revolutionary thinker could possibly have dreamed up what was going on right now in Stalin's Moscow? Only a Russian; Bakunin's Russian name caught Grisha's eye. Bakunin was mad to start with, wasn't he? That only re-inforced the humor of it all. Scanning the monument for other Russian names, he suddenly stopped and laughed more maniacally, for this monument had been erected in 1913 to celebrate the tercentenary of the House of Roma-nov. After the revolution, in 1918, it had been reconstructed as a monument to revolutionary thinkers, with Lenin him-self choosing the names. The Romanovs had been erased, in life as well as in stone, but of any name that had been or was on the tetrahedron, it was Romanov, the murdered Nicholas himself, who might have predicted the Red Ter-ror. And he would have been right! A real revolutionary thinker, the last tsar!

Still chuckling, Grisha sat down on the nearest bench.

Suddenly his laughter was interrupted by a slight thump on his leg, and he turned away from the monument to find a small boy, perhaps five or six years old, staring up at him in perplexed curiosity. Rather anxiously, the child glanced at Grisha's feet. Grisha followed the child's gaze to discover the light hoop that had obviously been the source of the mild bump he had experienced. The little boy held the stick with which he had been rolling the hoop. Grisha bent to pick up the toy.

"Is this yours?" he asked.

The boy nodded, but hesitated to come closer.

"Don't you want it?"

Again the child nodded, knitting his eyebrows together. Something serious and spirited in the gesture attracted Grisha. Especially the seriousness; Grisha had never been very much at ease with children, nor they with him.

"Well, then take it," Grisha ordered good-naturedly.

"Yes, go ahead and take it," a pleasant voice interjected.

Grisha turned to find a handsome, gray-haired woman; she wore her threadbare clothing with a sense of style that suggested nonproletarian origins. These people were still to be found everywhere. Normally irritated by them, Grisha now smiled at her. As he was admiring her, he felt the hoop slip out of his hand.

"And say 'thank-you,' Pyotr," she insisted.

"Thank you," the child mouthed almost inaudibly.

"And please excuse the accident," the woman said in her lilting voice.

Grisha nodded affably. He wanted to say something that would keep the woman and boy there next to him, but he couldn't think of anything.

"Pyotr, is it? What do you want to be when you grow up?" he asked in a formal, stilted way.

Pyotr responded with his own discomfort, screwing up his face and shrugging at the same time.

"That's too far away on a day like this," the woman said playfully.

"I suppose so," Grisha agreed, because he enjoyed hearing the vibrant voice that seemed so much younger than the speaker. He really didn't understand why anything was far away on a day like this. His death seemed to be lurking right outside the garden gate—behind the Kremlin wall?— and might leap out to grab him at any moment.

"Why, it's simply glorious for this time of year. Just look at it!"

She bobbed her head and waved her arm in the direction of the trees, bushes, flowers, and lawns.

Grisha stared obediently but did not see what the gray-haired woman was talking about.

"Have you ever enjoyed the Alexandrovsky so?" she trilled.

Before Grisha could consider a reply, a small serious voice at his feet informed him, "*Babye leto!*"

"What?" Grisha asked, looking down at the child, who already was shrinking back, surprised at his own bold utterance.

"*Babye leto,*" she explained politely.

"Was he speaking to you?" Grisha asked, mildly perplexed.

"I hope not," the woman laughed gaily.

"No, I didn't mean—" Grisha stammered, feeling himself blush.

"He might have been, though," she said with good humor.

"No, I don't think so," Grisha mustered lamely.

"I was just explaining to Pyotr the special name for the wonderfully warm days in autumn—*babye leto*—the last blush of youth experienced by an older woman. And he wanted to share it with you."

Grisha nodded. "*Babye leto,*" he repeated slowly.

"Beautiful, isn't it?"

"Yes, I suppose it is," Grisha said thoughtfully.

"What doubt can there be? It makes it a blessing to be alive," she said.

It is a blessing to be here with you, Grisha thought. As for the *babye leto*—oh well, just being alive was a blessing. And how long would that last?

"Pyotr, run along, dear. Be careful not to harm the officers of state security."

Grisha smiled, a touch ruefully. The NKVD didn't need anyone else's help in destroying its own officers. Pyotr nodded and ran down the boulevard with childish abandon.

"They have a lot of energy at that age," Grisha said with a hint of envy.

"I'll say they do," she agreed, accepting the implications of his statement.

"*Babye leto,*" Grisha repeated, not wanting to lose her company.

"Yes," she said softly, then added in a normal tone, "I left my book on the bench," excusing herself.

"You had better keep an eye on it," he agreed and began walking over to the bench.

The woman quickly caught up to him. Slightly uncomfortable at his solicitude, she fell silent. At the bench, she reached over and picked up an old, frayed volume of what Grisha assumed must be a novel printed before the revolution. The gold letters on the cover had worn and faded into illegibility.

"Do you mind if I sit down?" Grisha asked, ignoring her motions to depart.

"Oh, no, not at all," she said, seating herself with dignity, placing the book on her lap.

Grisha sat, too, at a respectful distance.

"Pyotr seems to be quite a bright young boy. Serious, but brimming with energy," he said, aware that he was repeating himself.

"Thank you," she said with the echo of a trill in her lilting voice.

Even Grisha's awkwardness didn't spoil her enchantment with the child.

"I'm afraid I'm not very good with children," he confessed.

"Well, it wasn't your fault that he almost ran you over. Adults are still permitted to enjoy a garden, too," she said with the return of her vivacious tone.

"Yes," Grisha agreed seriously. "You see, I never had any."

"Oh," the woman muttered, politely acknowledging that she had heard the remark.

"I always thought we would, my wife and I—but we never did—and now it's too late," he admitted with unabashed self-pity.

"I'm sorry," the woman sympathized.

"Do you have any other grandchildren?" Grisha asked.

"No," the woman smiled sadly. "I don't have any grand-children."

"Oh," Grisha replied. "You seem so attached to him."

"I am. He's my son," the woman said with the hint of a smile that suggested she had been embarrassed by the misconception many times before.

In spite of himself, Grisha couldn't help looking closely at the gray hair and clear face. She was not young. Fifty-five at least.

"Excuse me," he said forthrightly.

She nodded quickly in acceptance. "Everyone thinks so. They would be fools not to."

Not knowing what to say, Grisha commented, "He's a lovely child. I envy you."

"You see, for many years we didn't have any children either, my husband and I. He was even considerably older than I am. We had long ago given up hope—and then, as if three decades had not gone by, there we were—expecting." She paused. "You can imagine how surprised we were. At first we simply couldn't believe it. It seemed so improbable. Even embarrassing at my age."

"You must have been very happy."

"Oh, yes, oh, yes." She smiled quietly in remembrance. "So happy."

Couples strolled past. Not far away, two small children played with a ball. More than their ineffectual pushes, their gurgling sounds seemed to propel the red sphere.

"Your husband must be very happy with such a special child," Grisha added graciously.

"Yes, he was. For the first year he was almost afraid to touch him. He called him 'our sacred doll.' Then"—

she paused—"when he wanted to hold him, it was already too late."

Grisha knew what was sure to follow; without turning toward her, he asked, "And where is he out there?"

"Solovki," she said.

He didn't want to look, for he knew what he would find: tears in her eyes. But he did look, because he wanted to see those eyes, their beauty and their accusation, for Colonel Shwartzman had sent many to the Solovetsky Islands in the White Sea, from whose monastic prison none returned. When he looked, however, he was surprised. Neither tears nor accusation greeted him, only a plea for help. Help for her husband, Pyotr's father. Grisha did not understand how a man could survive the agony of separation from such a wife and child.

"His name is—" the woman was saying, but Grisha shook his head, and her voice dropped off.

"There was a time many years ago when I would not have helped you. Then I could have. Now that I would like to help, it is too late. I cannot. I . . . I shall not even make it to Solovki. I can't even deliver a message."

"Oh, I'm sorry," she murmured.

Grisha nodded. He, too, was sorry.

"Is Solovetsky as bad as they say?" she whispered, her voice husky with fear.

Grisha nodded but could not look at her. He heard her catch her breath, and he nervously began to straighten his tunic, but quickly stopped, as he felt the shame of his uniform on his flesh.

"You must believe that if I could help you, I would," he implored, but as he did so, he really didn't know whether it was true. He wished it were, and it was very important that she believe it.

"I hope your wife has you with her for many years," she said kindly.

At the mention of his wife, Grisha smiled wryly.

"Isn't she with you?" she asked in gentle solicitude.

"After a fashion," he answered enigmatically.

She respected his reticence, and they sat quietly. Grisha stood up.

"I had better be going," he announced.

She nodded as if appreciating his having spent precious time with her, given his busy schedule. Then she asked, "Why were you laughing so heartily by the monument just now?"

"There was a time many years ago when revolutionary thinkers brought joy to my soul," he explained.

"I see, *babye leto*," she said quietly, with her own sad understanding of the term.

"Yes." He nodded to her ever so slightly, as if they had a set of gestures that only they could understand.

As he departed along the path that led deeper into the garden, Pyotr came running by him, his hoop rolling along with a metallic swish as if it were a great scythe whose deadly blade reached all the way to the Solovetsky Islands in the frigid north seas. As he entered the linden boulevard he heard an insistent young voice calling, "Citizen Colonel!" and he turned back to find Pyotr racing up to him with the brown cloth bag. Breathing heavily, with small beads of sweat rapidly forming on his temples, the child proffered the object.

"Citizen Colonel, you forgot your bag," the boy announced.

"Thank you. Yes, I did," Grisha said, taking it.

"You're welcome," the boy responded and turned to sprint back to his elderly mother.

"Good-bye," Grisha said.

"Be careful, I think there's a bottle inside," Pyotr informed him, his brows knitted with the burden of serious information.

"I'll try, Pyotr," Grisha said with dolorous resignation that the boy neither heard nor saw, since he was already darting down the tree-lined path.

CHAPTER EIGHT

GRISHA CHOSE ANOTHER BENCH UNDER THE INTERLACED branches of the lime trees. Placing the wine next to him, he sat down. Not ready for any more encounters, he wanted to savor the one he had just had. Grisha had told the truth: no one returns from the Solovetsky Islands. If Pyotr weren't already an orphan, he certainly would be. Nothing less than a miracle could save his father, and yet, Grisha mused, if it weren't for a miracle, Pyotr wouldn't be in this world now. Grisha, however, couldn't find much solace in that. After all, if his family had used up its quota, how could Pyotr expect another miracle? And even miracles had limitations; the secret police permitted none. Whoever her husband was—most likely a tsarist officer, perhaps a guards officer; the woman was very aristocratic in the most natural manner—he was as good as dead.

But, again indulging in self-pity, Grisha envied the anonymous recipient of the miracle called Pyotr. What family did Grisha have? His wife, Rachel Leah, in the closet—"Is she still with you?" "After a fashion."—and what a degenerate condition she was in!

Grisha looked around at the lush greens of the lime and linden trees, the lawns still a dark healthy swath and the deep golden flowers hinting at the autumnal harvest only weeks, perhaps no more than days away, when the cold would bring the vernal warmth to a sudden, definitive end. Grisha himself couldn't revel in the *babye leto;* he evoked it more as tribute to the gray-haired woman. There were no beautiful days in which to die, at least not for him, not yet. Not every autumn has a *babye leto,* and unfortunately, not every revolution has one either. The Glorious Red Revolution had needed one for some time. He must have been an anomalous sight, an NKVD colonel laughing lustily in front of the Monument to Revolutionary Thinkers. Had she understood that Grisha really wanted to help her, or had she realized the truth? Where had it all gone wrong? Lenin himself had chosen the names for the monument!

It all was very confusing, and part of him—Colonel Hershel Shwartzman?—didn't want to think about it. What had happened, after all, had to have happened, hadn't it? There was a revolutionary logic, based on revolutionary necessity, that had started it all. Another part of him—Grisha?—was curious as to how it had all come to this. Indeed he, the son of a Volhynian Jewish merchant, was seeking refuge under the spire of the Kremlin's Trinity Tower of Russian Orthodoxy. Why hadn't they changed the name of the tower? Was there something in that? He wondered: was there a deep insidious clerical plot that had undermined the revolution? Stalin should be told of this.

Stalin? That was the madness he was trying to hide from. He would love to escape that murderous madness, but there was no escape, only a temporary refuge in the tsar's gardens under the tsar's wall, under the Holy Russian Father's Trinity Tower. Did the Great Genius of Humanity, Joseph Stalin, have to be told that? He knew all—or did he? Was Stalin "they," or was he their prisoner as well? Why should Stalin be concerned with only a simple colonel in the NKVD? How could he be concerned with millions of simple people?

Grisha knew they were arresting by quota now. Could a nation have so many enemies? Soviet Russia was not just a dog chasing its tail; with the aid of the state security services, Soviet Russia had the misfortune of being the dog who had successfully caught its tail in its sharp-toothed muzzle and was devouring itself, past the tail by name and into the muscle of the hindquarters! How could it chase anything else? What if the German fascists attacked?

Grisha had welcomed Stalin's accession, he admitted that. Stalin was a decisive manager at a time when things lacked focus. Stalin had launched the collectivization of agriculture. Millions of kulaks had been shot, millions driven from their land. Famine followed, and millions in the villages and towns died. Grisha, too, had referred to collectivization as "the logic of the struggle," but wasn't it a daunting logic? The people weren't ready for collectivization. The only way to force them into it was to shoot them, and shoot them they did, just as they had shot the tsar. But the tsar had deserved it! It was a shame they couldn't bring the tsar back to life and shoot him over and over again instead of the kulaks.

Although they couldn't resurrect the tsar, they had imbued him with some great life force that tainted all "former people" in any way related to tsarist Russia. The tsarist plague emanating from the Romanov grave was so powerful that it infected the children of "class enemies." What would be Pyotr's future as the son of aristocrats, son of a tsarist officer? Grisha himself had succeeded in obliterating his bourgeois past because Russian Volynia had been ceded to the Polish Republic after the World War. Later, in the Civil War with Cossack regiments, Grisha had fought over the area, only to be driven back by Pilsudski. The bitter loss of Grisha's home province had probably saved his life in the Stalinist years—until now. It didn't, however, prevent Svetkov from taunting him about Rachel Leah, his bourgeois wife who sat in the closet waiting. Who could know what she was waiting for? She had been there so long, she herself probably no longer had any idea.

And to think that he had married Rachel Leah because of a bench! Now he was a fugitive on one in the park. Over thirty years ago, however, he had been a fugitive under a synagogue bench in that backwater of Krimsk that had laid him low. Well, Grisha thought, that's some progress: in thirty-three years he had managed to rise from the floor to the furniture. But in Krimsk it had been coincidence that the young talmudist Yechiel Katzman had led him to the refuge of the empty prayerhouse. As a young Marxist revolutionary fleeing the tsar's police, Grisha had awakened there to realize that he had slept in the very house of worship that his own father had offered as a gift to the Krimsker Rebbe. The rebbe, however, refused all gifts, both large and small, and when Grisha's father had dedicated the building in the rebbe's absence, the great brass chandelier had crashed upon him in lethal bourgeois tragedy.

Grisha had forced himself to overcome his childish

fear by returning to sleep in the prayerhouse. And Grisha, too, had almost died in the very same place, when the peasants in an attempted pogrom set alight the great wooden structure. Their incendiary clamor had awakened the sleeping Grisha; trapped in the flames, he had plucked the holy Torah scroll from the Ark of the Law. Fleeing the fiery vestibule, Grisha had burst into the arms of the Krimsker Rebbe, who was rushing inside the blazing building to save the very same Torah scroll. Escaping certain death, they emerged spinning like a top with the scroll clutched between them. The peasants, mistaking the singed, fiery figure of Grisha for the devil himself, had fled in fear. In some magical way, the Krimsker Rebbe had identified Grisha as his father's son, Hershel the son of Chaim Shwartzman. The rebbe declared that Grisha had received the Torah of Mount Sinai, and in order to maintain the brilliance of the holy sparks (heaven forbid they should turn into cold ash), he awarded Grisha Rachel Leah, his pure daughter, as his wife.

And the very next day, instead of Yechiel the young talmudist, Grisha, still aching from his burns, married her. Within weeks the Krimsker Rebbe and his rebbitzen departed for America, whereas Grisha, his wounds healing, returned to the Communist struggle against the tsar. Grisha assumed that he and Rachel Leah would separate, returning to their own intense, all-absorbing worlds, but he had not appreciated his new bride's dedication and madness. Although as a dutiful wife she had physically followed him into his world, spiritually she inhabited only her own. Their separation was not a possibility, because she would not leave him. For thirty-three years she had followed him as if he were a straying prophet who one day would return to her

Torah and, presumably, to Krimsk. Grisha shook his head in wonder; when it came to believing in historical necessity, Rachel Leah made the Bolsheviks seem like the atheists they claimed to be.

As Grisha sat in the fading light of the Alexandrovsky Gardens, he felt a surge of sorrow that Rachel Leah couldn't enjoy such a pastoral scene. But for her there was no *babye leto*. Had there been, Grisha would have left her. Comrades had intimated that a crazed religious wife was hindering his career. No doubt she had—might he not have been Svetkov's superior? Grisha had always silenced his critics by asking what they suggested he do with her. Then he would suggest that if nothing else, he was loyal: loyal to the revolution, loyal to the party, and loyal to victims of bourgeois oppression, namely his wife. He believed that the opiate of religion had dulled her senses beyond repair. Some day Soviet security would triumph, and there would be appropriate facilities, but until then he could not desert her.

What would her fate be after they took him? Well, what was her fate now? And what was his? Sitting on a park bench watching old people with young children filing past toward the gates. Young couples rose from the benches and, hand in hand, followed the rays of the sun out of the garden. Their absorbed expressions grew more radiant as the sun itself failed. Grisha suddenly felt very old, as if he had just discovered that he had been slowly petrifying on the park bench and had now become one more lifeless artifact. The lovers strolled past the silent trees, the metal lampposts, the stone benches, and the fossilized Chekist. On the monument the revolutionaries' names were chiseled in stone. On the bench, the revolutionary had ossified into obdurate rock, the petrified colonel. Even the stone of the NKVD has eyes!

Grisha recalled asking himself in the Lubyanka, Is anyone screwing in Russia? Who are these young couples? Does the NKVD know? Grisha wondered why he was so concerned about that. It had something to do with Stalin. With a rush of shame, Grisha felt Dmitri Cherbyshev returning with his leering filth. The man should be shot! Grisha should send his confession by special messenger directly to Yezhov, head of the NKVD. Perhaps Yezhov would also shoot Svetkov. And Grisha, too, for that matter.

After all the men Grisha had shot, seen shot, and ordered to be shot, it remained a great mystery that he should be shot. Of course there was an abundance of people who wanted to shoot him, but that any one of them should succeed in such a base desire seemed unbelievable. Rational Marxist that he was, Grisha didn't believe it. The greater the probability of such an unbelievable event, the greater Stalin's failure—his murderous tyranny. How could a state have so many enemies! Stalin wreaked havoc in Russia. The Great Teacher didn't appreciate Grisha's efforts on his and Russia's behalf.

Grisha recalled that fateful night so many years ago when the Krimsker Rebbe had warned Grisha's friend, the young talmudist Yechiel Katzman, "Do not underestimate evil!" When Yechiel had reported the rebbe's words, Grisha had naively thought they applied only to the tsar. His crazy old father-in-law had been correct. His warning applied to everyone. In spite of their Bolshevik vigilance, somewhere, somehow, evil had entered and turned the Glorious Red Revolution into today's terror.

Sitting anonymously in the gathering darkness, sheltered beneath the myriad nameless leaves that had outlived
the Romanovs of Russia—and would survive him, too—
Grisha could admit the harsh truth: Lenin had created the
Cheka. Lenin had appealed in 1918—so long ago, and yet so
recently—to "purge the land of all kinds of insects." Lenin
had authorized more than arbitrary arrests; in the pseudo-
plots in 1919, people were shot without trials. How Lenin
had hated the Social Revolutionaries and the Mensheviks!
He hadn't hesitated in "purging the insects." Pyotr's father
was an insect. Pyotr's mother was another, and unfortunately, revolutionary logic made Pyotr one, too. And now
the exterminators themselves had become the insects within
the heavy walls of the Lubyanka, crawling forth in the shape
of Orlov's black Fiat. The Romanovs had grown parasitic,
and the tsarist obelisk at the entrance to the garden stood
like a sterile hive. Lenin had introduced a new swarm:
Marx the queen, Lenin the worker, the Cheka the willing
swarm; but now—the honey was lost but not the sting!
Stalin was brutal; no one could resist.

Lenin had preached that without the state security
service, the Soviet regime could not exist, and he was right.
What Lenin preached, Stalin practiced, elevating the exis-
tential doctrine to the august heights that the state exists
"for" the security services. Whom does the NKVD protect?
Why, the NKVD, of course. Still, Grisha was confused; absurd as the logic of the NKVD was, he still couldn't fathom
the necessity of his own death. A death, he understood,
that had already been determined. A death he did not have
the courage to face. Above all, a death he did not have the
courage to resist. No one resisted. Grisha was wearing a

pistol this very minute—why hadn't he shot Dmitri Cher-byshev through his ridiculous eyes!—but he knew that he would never draw the weapon in his defense. The NKVD believed that they were arresting dangerous saboteurs, but the truth was, no one resisted. On the contrary, people rushed hysterically to surrender their guns. Without them, some continued to run about in frenzy, but none ever resisted arrest. Others calmed down, their manic hysteria settling into debilitating fear. Immobilized, they could barely open the front door. The security agents had to pound on the door until they woke the victim from his stupor. Fearlessly nursing their battered knuckles, they rushed in to arrest the vicious saboteur in the dim light.

With the silent memory of fists flying about a wooden door like moths assaulting a candle, Grisha dozed off.

CHAPTER NINE

HE AWOKE WITH A START. RELIEVED TO DISCOVER THAT he was in the Alexandrovsky Gardens and not in a cell of the Lubyanka, Grisha felt embarrassed, even humiliated that he, a colonel of the NKVD, was snoozing on a park bench like a derelict. Hoping that he had not been recognized, he jumped up and, on legs stiff from sleep, hurried out of the garden.

Rushing along the dark path, he wondered how long he had dozed. He crossed under the crenellated bridge that connected the Trinity Gate with Manege Square. Once, the Alexandrovsky Gardens had been a moat; the night shadows under the arches were as dark as any deep, still water could have been. Grisha hurried through the thick, suffocating shadows into the middle garden and turned right toward the steps that climbed up to the street and the small white stone Kutafya Tower that guarded the entrance to the ancient bridge. A large crowd was bustling out of the subway station. Grisha witnessed their animated arrival with relief; they were returning home from work. It couldn't be very late. Their rushing feet thumped the pavement in a cacophony of energetic taps, muffling the dense warmth of the *babye leto* night. Grisha, a stranger, envied them their bold anonymity. Did they know summer would end? In the dense air, Grisha felt as if all summer were compressed into a rich suffocation of days. He couldn't move as fast as the anonymous ones who rushed from the subways. The old, heavy dark brick walls of the Kremlin with the sealed Trinity Gate, the deserted Trinity Bridge, and the desolate solid white stones of the Kutafya guardhouse made more sense than the subway. The old oppressive pride, tsarist and splendid, stood in dumb silence, a funereal monument to a bourgeois world. The new pride of the subway—how they had torn up these royal gardens for the steel bands of the Sokolniki line!—served everyone at a modest price, as its tunnels stretched under all Moscow like long, vaulted graves, endless in either direction, proletarian crypts with burials every two or three minutes. And the Lubyanka could fill them—the Lubyanka would fill them—but no, thought Grisha, the NKVD plucked their victims from among the witless bodies who descended willingly into the subways. The NKVD ghouls pulled them from the proletarian grave only to suck their blood and serve them chilled in Siberia. The subway was a preliminary stage, an unannounced test, administered to the passive population.

No one resisted, least of all Grisha. No, he had escaped from the innards of the NKVD's necrophagous bug. He rushed up the stairs to the street, where he sought refuge near the white stones guarding the drawbridge to the Kremlin. Although the ancient fortress now sheltered Stalin, he was a mere blasphemer inside among its venerable tyrants.

The Kremlin belonged to the tsars, to the Church—after all, at the other end of the narrow bridge rose the Trinity Tower. How could an officer of the NKVD linger in the shadow of the Okhrana, the tsarist secret police, violating Section 13 of Article 58?

Turning his back on both cenotaphs—tsardom's Kremlin and Stalin's sepulchral subway—Grisha hurried across the still street separating the Manege from the Alexandrovsky Gardens.

By the great exhibition hall, Grisha suddenly remembered the brown bag. Where was the wine? But what did he need the wine for? He had intentionally forgotten it earlier, only to have Pyotr return it to him, warning him to be careful with the bottle. Grisha had said that he would try. Hadn't he told Pyotr's mother that he would have helped them if he could? Each tall, stately column of the Exhibition Hall—as noble and stately as guards' officers—reproached him for his counterrevolutionary infatuation with the "former people." The guards' horses ate better than the proletariat!

With a stab of pain, he remembered the kulaks, who no longer ate at all. Grisha turned and began to retrace his steps toward the base of the Kremlin wall. He walked quickly, as if he had somewhere to go, some pressing appointment with Svetkov, but he didn't, did he? He walked faster. He wasn't quite running away; he was afraid of the subway entrance. It seemed to beckon like a bottomless pit. To regain the wine, Grisha would have to pass by the subway twice. He was running out of chances.

CHAPTER TEN

KEEPING FAITH WITH PYOTR, AND PYOTR'S MOTHER, too—how could anyone still have such a lilting voice in Stalin's Russia, much less a former person?—Grisha had survived his return trip. With the wine bottle tucked carefully under his arm, he slowed his pace and began strolling along Vozdvizhenie Boulevard away from the Kremlin and toward his home in the Arbat district.

The warm silky romantic night caressed all of Moscow like the sensuous, perfumed air of a Spanish song. Grisha attributed it to the counterrevolutionary tendencies of the climate. The NKVD would find out who was responsible and clap them in the Lubyanka, where they would learn to "sing" all right, vividly describing counterrevolutionary visits to foreign climates.

Arriving at Arbat Square, he paused to see whether he could discover any parked cars that might be waiting to follow him down the narrow Arbat Street. If there were, where would he go? Around in circles, following the rings of Moscow? But no suspicious automobiles filled with dark figures huddled along the curb.

Just as he had steeled himself earlier in the day to enter the car in the Lubyanka courtyard, he now surrendered to a debilitating fatalism. He turned off the main street and stolidly pursued one of the picturesque lanes to his own front door. No one emerged from the shadows to greet him. The small, quiet street slumbered as if the time were long past midnight.

Most evenings, when he was carrying something, he would nudge the great plank door open with his shoulder, but tonight, fearing to turn his back on the entrance, he leaned on the lock with the key still inside. Its inertia was so great that at first he imagined that someone on the other side was holding it closed. Finally it began moving, and Grisha saw that no one was there. Only a small light that he had seen from outside burned in the foyer.

An interior door opened as he closed the front one.

"Good evening, Comrade Colonel," Pangolin said.

"Good evening, Comrade Pangolin," he answered.

The old man always spoke to him deferentially, but Grisha could hear Comrade Pangolin's anxiety. Something was wrong.

"How did everything go today, Comrade?" Grisha asked confidently.

The old man shuffled slightly without answering. Although stockily built, he seemed to bend slightly under the burden of the question or even under the pressure of the light that was flowing downward through the open doorway behind him.

"Did you have any trouble getting the food?" Grisha asked.

Although Grisha ate most of his meals in the NKVD commissary, Pangolin purchased the little food his wife needed. It was part of their agreement and had generally worked well.

"I got what she needed. Some bread and some cheese," Pangolin answered.

Stepping closer to the befuddled old man, Grisha placed a comforting hand on his friend's arm. "Pangolin, what seems to be the problem?" he asked solicitously.

Pangolin blinked. "There's a letter for you," he said ominously.

"Well, let's see it."

"I don't have it," Pangolin said guiltily. "I told them that I take all your mail, but they said they wouldn't give it to me."

"Who are 'they'?" Grisha asked.

"People from your office, I think. They weren't wearing uniforms."

"Four?" Grisha asked.

Pangolin nodded.

"I told them you authorize me to accept all mail and messages, but they said that wasn't good enough."

Pangolin shook his head nervously, as if he had failed his benefactor.

"That's all right," Grisha assured him. "It's not your fault. Some of the younger staff are too enthusiastic."

The old man didn't appear to be comforted.

"Well, if it's important, they'll be back, and I'm home

now, so don't worry," Grisha said. "Good night," he added, and turned toward the steps.

"It's upstairs," Pangolin called after him.

Grisha stopped.

"What is?"

"The letter. They tacked it to the door. They warned me that I had better not touch it."

CHAPTER ELEVEN

SINCE PANGOLIN WAS WATCHING, GRISHA CLIMBED THE elegant, curved staircase with an air of great confidence. Had one of his downstairs tenants not been present, he would have quickly run his hand across his tunic front in preparation for what he might encounter at the top of the stairs. His military bearing was appropriate, for the staircase was indeed very grand—too much so for the townhouse, as if the railroad magnate Mironov, its builder, had purloined it from one of his own stations. It seemed at least two sizes too big and too elegant for the otherwise modest mansion. In his more philosophical moods, when he found Marxist meaning in the world, Grisha had very much enjoyed the steps' grandeur, for they seemed to symbolize the only legitimate historical contribution of bourgeois capitalism—the transition to the higher Communist society. In the former Mironov mansion, Grisha felt most at home on these steps. So, too, no doubt would have Mironov himself, for the first floor had been partitioned off into three apartments, and the upper floor was in a state of barren decay.

Only the staircase with its marble balustrade remained the same, and even it had changed at the top. As if announcing the new order, a wooden partition abruptly cut off the graceful ascent.

In recent weeks, standing in front of his ill-fitting wooden door while fumbling for the private key, Grisha had thought that at least the capitalists had left a staircase. What had his own revolution produced?—a squalid barricade? Not only the Lubyanka had been remodeled. Tonight, however, his attention turned to the communication that the buffoonish Svetkov had sent him. Only a small light-bulb on the lower landing cast any light up into the walled-off gloom, enabling Grisha faintly to detect a white oblong envelope on the door. It didn't seem to be the usual kind from the office. No doubt Svetkov had found something special for him. Grisha suspected that it had something to do with Rosh Hashanah. Svetkov could never abandon a joke before he had run it into the ground. Grisha tucked the brown cloth bag under his elbow and fished out the key. Feeling for the lock with his left hand, he inserted the key with his right.

Not until he managed to open the door and switch on the light did he see that the letter bore foreign stamps, from the United States of America. As he reached to take it from the door, his knees weakened and wobbled slightly; he tightened his elbow on the wine bottle, which had started to slide from his grip. Thinking better of his attempt, he put the brown bag on a chair. In Stalin's Russia any foreign letter constituted a mortal danger—Article 57, Section 3. His mouth twisting slightly open as if he were about to scream, he pulled the envelope off the door. The liberated tack sprang forth and fell onto the floor. Grisha moved directly under the naked lightbulb and brought the envelope up to his eyes. It was addressed to him personally. He turned it over, morbidly fearing news of death when he saw the return address and the name of the sender, Yaakov Moshe Finebaum, his father-in-law, the Krimsker Rebbe.

Anxiously scanning the opening lines, he relaxed as he realized that his father-in-law was writing that his mother-in-law was in good health. No one had died. Slowly, with increasing curiosity, he read on, and what he read so astounded him that he could not even scream.

My Dear Son-in-Law,

Your mother-in-law, my esteemed rebbetzin, may her days be goodly and long, has asked me to write to you, dear children, about the Messiah. Alas, I must inform you that he has not come. We are surrounded by impure fakes and wicked impostors.

Reb Zelig, whom you may remember from the Angel of Death Synagogue in Krimsk, has died, may he rest in peace. I invite you, dear Hershel, to fill his position as my sexton in St. Louis. I am left without a driver, and there is no one to say kaddish for the tsar. If you do not know how to drive, you can learn when you arrive here. You must however begin saying kaddish for the tsar at once. At once! You and your sordid Bolshevik associates ran to spill his blood. At least he was a tsar; he was regal. You can't forget the uniforms: an intimation of the King's porphyra—for Israel is the royal purple garment. What do you have in his place? A common joke!

The New Year will soon arrive. You must repent, for Rosh Hashanah is the Day of Judgment. Fear not, for I shall tell you the secret of Rosh Hashanah: creation. The rest of the year one must make a tremendous, difficult effort to change. However, since Adam was created on Rosh Hashanah, the day itself brings one to penitence. One can become a new man. On this day the Holy One looked into his holy Torah and created the world. You saved that Torah. Now let that Torah save you on Rosh Hashanah.

All my blessings for the New Year. May you and your wife be inscribed and sealed in the Book of Life.

Yours,
Yaakov Moshe Finebaum

P.S. You're not too old to learn to fly, either. If you have a leather jacket and scarf, bring them.

The letter slid from Grisha's paralyzed hand, and he uttered a low, choking groan as if he were being eviscerated. His mortal "uggh" brought no response from inside the large armoire. Grisha's head slumped onto the table. A great black cloud seemed to encompass him. He lay that way for some minutes. Grisha himself had no sense of time, nor any sense of breathing either. What he did sense in the blackness was the nonexistence that prefigured and surrounded his death. Then, slowly at first, he choked for breath, and the black began to loosen its dark grip. As Grisha gasped for air, the dark dissipated, giving way to a dull brown that, fueled by his furious anger, then turned a fiery red.

Hammering his fist on the letter, Grisha sat up, muttering, "No one died? No one died?" Then, staring across the table at the ornate, heavy wardrobe a few feet beyond, he called, "That crazy old man is trying to kill me."

He stared at the letter in horror as if it were a dagger dripping with his own blood. "Your father has murdered me!" he whispered in stupefied, almost unbelieving outrage.

"Do you hear, Rachel Leah, that madman has killed me. All the way from America, he has put a bullet in my head!" This last he uttered with no small amazement.

"The lunatic has managed to do Stalin's work for him."

Grisha felt the final swirl of the carousel gather him in its dizzying spiral. He had the frightening thought that he might not be thrown off but instead sucked toward the center, where he would disappear like a small bug spinning down the drain. Life had more than one surprise! His previous image of destruction—so well understood—suddenly seemed normal, even reasonable. Who was the Krimsker Rebbe to be inflicting such a strange and dreadful fate upon him? An image of the froglike Krimsker Rebbe surfaced. The enigmatic madman was standing with his hands on a long gear controlling the carousel. He threatened to speed it up, spinning it into water. It would drain itself into a central drop and then evaporate altogether. So it wasn't Stalin: it was the rebbe! At first Grisha laughed at the incredible comparison, but there did seem to be something comparable. The rebbe did exactly what he wanted and didn't explain himself to anyone. The world, or at least the world of his hasidim, ran after him, almost deifying him and idealizing his every action. Grisha wondered whether anyone abused his father-in-law the way Dmitri Cherbyshev straddled Stalin, and as soon as he thought it, he was flooded with anger and shame.

"I should have shot the bastard! I should have blown the beast's brains out!" he wailed in despair. "I should have killed him," he bellowed.

From the depths of the wardrobe, a thin, reedy voice pronounced, "How Father loves God."

"What?" Grisha asked, for the voice was muffled by the door, and heaven knew what else she had dragged in there with her. There had been a time when she sat buried in books—but since the summer she sat covered with every towel in the apartment. He had tried hiding a few for his personal use, but as if she had a sixth sense, she had unerringly found them.

"What?" he repeated, but he had heard her, and it was just as well, because she wasn't repeating the remark. She just sat muffled in towels. At night he was often reduced to wiping his hands on his tunic!

"Rachel Leah, I wasn't talking about your father," he called to the closed cabinet door. "I was talking about a prisoner in the Lubyanka!"

The words "loves God" faintly reached him. Grisha wondered whether she had heard his explanation, and if so, whether she had understood. It wasn't very clear to him how much she understood about what he was doing or about Pangolin and his wife when they brought her food.

"Not your father!" he repeated, although not loud enough for her to hear.

Not your father, although he is a lunatic. I'm not too old to learn to fly! I should bring a leather jacket and a scarf and learn to fly! The man must be stark raving mad. And

writing to tell me to say "kaddish for the tsar" . . . and calling Stalin "a common joke" was like pulling the trigger.

"How could he?" Grisha whispered aloud, but he knew
how he could. The rebbe was mad. Where did he think
Grisha was, that he could write such things? Certainly the
rebbe knew something of Stalin's Russia. The rebbe couldn't
be deceived by Bolshevik propaganda. Others, maybe, but
not him. Did the rebbe really want to kill him? Was the
rebbe really mad?

Grisha picked up the letter. As for the Messiah not having come, the rebbe could not be more correct. Grisha
knew all about "the impure fakes and wicked impostors."
Wasn't Stalin one? Wasn't Grisha himself one? The rebbe
would never know how fortunate he was that his Messiah
had not come. Waiting was the best part. Lenin had not
been the Messiah; Stalin had not been the Messiah; but
what was worse, all of Russia had to pretend they were.

At least the rebbe didn't pretend to be the Messiah. His
father-in-law's promise of "a new man" frightened Grisha.
He had had more than enough of new men for one lifetime. The rebbe was promising a new, private spiritual man,
not a social creature dependent on an entire society. Probably the rebbe's new man was better than Stalin's—how
could he be worse?—but Grisha didn't feel as though he
had the energy to make the acquaintance of any new men,
even one he could believe in.

Reb Zelig had died! Grisha's own father had hired Reb
Zelig as the sexton of the synagogue he had built in
Krimsk, the Angel of Death. Lenin himself couldn't have
picked a better name for a religious institution. How many
years ago? Thirty? No, it would have to be closer to fifty.

His father had died in the Angel of Death, and Grisha almost had as well, in that blazing inferno when he had saved the Torah and been awarded the rebbe's daughter as a prize. Grisha, charred by the fire—fueled by the need for a father? sparked by lust?—lapsed from his Marxism and accepted her. She had trembled beneath his touch. And now? She was mad. Thirty-three years later she sat childless and mad inside Mironov's armoire. And ironically he, Grisha, too, had been sentenced to die by the Angel of Death after all. Reb Zelig had died, the rebbe wrote in his letter asking Grisha to replace him, and what a letter! "Say kaddish for the tsar"—"sordid Bolsheviks"—Stalin "a common joke!" Why, a neophyte investigator in the Lubyanka could sentence a man to death ten times over for every phrase. Religious conspiracy ("I shall tell you the secret of Rosh Hashanah"), serving the Okhrana ("you can't forget the uniforms"), conspiracy with a foreign power and planning to escape ("You're not too old to learn to fly"—what in the world did the rebbe mean by that?). Wittingly or not, the rebbe had sentenced him to death, all right. Mad or sane, it made no difference. The rebbe had killed him, his own son-in-law!

Grisha felt tired and very noble, like an innocent victim, and he felt the need to relieve himself, too. He pushed the letter away and rose from the table. Staggering through the dark, empty apartment—Mironov must have had quite a home before he was shot—Grisha mused that in pre-revolutionary times a condemned man was entitled to a last meal, whereas in modern times his own last worldly pleasure was to urinate. So much for the socialism of his youth, he thought as he groped his way through the darkness. He heard the sound of an automobile engine growling in the street below and froze in panic. If the lemur was imaginary, the lion with its sharp claws and teeth was real. Grisha held his breath as the automobile continued down the quiet, curved street. He began to breathe again. What did he care if they went to collect another victim? It wasn't him.

Still quivering with fear, he didn't switch on a light. Standing in the dark, he could feel the dampness of the rotten walls. Last winter Rachel Leah had left the sink faucet running one winter day when he had gone to Leningrad, and two rooms had been completely destroyed before he had returned. Who could covet such an apartment? Although he could feel the wet on the wall, he stood unsuccessfully attempting his final leak. The prowling car had paralyzed him. He was thankful that the darkness hid his dry humiliation. Alone with himself and his shame, he realized that the seed of a strange thought was beginning to germinate in the dark, humid room. Before he could articulate it, its inception seemed to unlock his fears, and he began to relieve himself. Quieted, he listened to the sound of the singular stream in the darkness. It was what it was, no more, no less.

Staggering back through Mironov's rooms, Grisha felt both weighed down and unburdened. The NKVD automobile would come for him, and "they" would take him to his death. Mad or not, it wasn't the Krimsker Rebbe who was responsible. Grisha didn't want to admit it, but he realized who "they" were. "They" was really "he," and "he" was Colonel Hershel Shwartzman, and Colonel Hershel Shwartzman was Grisha himself. He hadn't been surprised when he had shot the Whites. That was a revolutionary necessity! He had not been pleased, but he was educated about the necessity of eliminating the kulaks. The death of others didn't frighten him, but he had been stunned into disbelief at his own impending execution. Now he even understood the revolutionary necessity of that. He was no better than the others: the Bukharinists, the left oppositionists, the Mensheviks, the kulaks, the Whites. The whole thing had been murderously wrong from the start. Gasparov had been right in his defiance, and Cherbyshev had been right, too! Stalin is us. We are Stalin. Yes, Stalin was a brute, but he wasn't the first. Stalin was the product of a necessity, an absolutely unnecessary necessity. There had been no necessity for the revolution. The mad revolution of the carousel would destroy Grisha, too. Neither the Krimsker Rebbe nor his letter would kill him. It wasn't even Stalin alone, as he would have everyone believe. Grisha himself had been operating the carousel!

Grisha almost hoped to hear the sound of the black Fiat so he would be forced to stop thinking such thoughts, but no purring motor muffled the sound of his weary feet dragging across Mironov's parquet floors. He knew that he was responsible. The secret was out. The rebbe had told him a secret, too—a secret of creation. Maybe this Jewish secret might have been Grisha's. No, probably not, but it might have been poor Rachel Leah's. Who knew what secrets she was guarding in that wardrobe on the night of Rosh Hashanah? All along, he had been sure that he had done her a great favor by not abandoning her when her primitive religious fervor was an insult to progress and a threat to his career. Now he wondered if there was room in the wardrobe for two.

He listened carefully for the telltale sounds of Stalin's new men in their old car, but he couldn't detect the rumble of a motor, the hum of a rubber tire, the pop of a car door. Nothing. What was left? Grisha knew.

He circled through the empty rooms until he arrived in the hallway. The barricade at the top of the steps seemed flimsier than ever before and uglier, too. There was no seeking shelter behind its raw, unfinished boards. He collected the brown cloth bag and returned to their room. Like all the others, it, too, was Mironov's, but at least they lived in this one. He opened the sack and placed the bottle of wine on the table; its brownish red bubbles gurgled up to the top in quick, darting certainty. Methodically he turned to the sideboard for Rachel Leah's candlesticks. The two knobby silver objects filled his hands with an imposing weight— purposeful, menacing, and dusty. He looked around for a towel or cloth. Finding none, he slowly wiped them with the bottom of his tunic, but their protuberances were covered with leaves in relief, and the dust sought refuge in the crevices and nooks. There was no time for the official NKVD garment to do the job properly. He placed the pair toward the center of the long, large table. On the same grand scale, they graced it handsomely.

In the candle box he searched for tall, new tapers, but because of the numerous power failures, there were only used ones. He chose two almost new candles, although one had dark black smears from a poor wick. It would have to do.

From the drawer he removed the coarse loaves Pangolin had acquired and put them on the simple wooden cutting board near the head of the table. He remembered that they should be covered with a cloth, but he didn't bother searching for one. They would lie bare. He put the simple bread knife near the loaves. He checked his preparations. Ah yes, he needed something for the wine. Glancing futilely at the sideboard where he had found Rachel Leah's candlesticks, he remembered that he no longer had his silver kiddush cup. That, too, had been a wedding gift from the rebbe and rebbetzin. What had happened to it? He couldn't quite remember, but at the time it had seemed insignificant. Hadn't Rachel Leah stuffed it into his pack when he rode with the Cossacks? Had he given it to a wounded comrade dying of thirst? Had it fallen clanking to the ground as he dashed from a nameless town under enemy fire? Had he traded it for boots? It must have been long ago. He could no longer remember, and he didn't really want to know. Sometimes forgetting was merciful, but he wished it weren't so long, long ago.

He took a plain glass tumbler and set it and the bottle next to the bread. Moving a wooden chair from the side where he usually sat, he placed it at the head for himself. At the opposite end of the table, he placed a chair for his wife. It was impossibly distant, but that was the only setting that seemed appropriate for the festal inauguration of the New Year, Rosh Hashanah.

All was ready. No, not quite. After she lit the candles, he would recite the kiddush over the cup of wine, sanctifying the Day of Judgment. On the shelf he found Rachel Leah's prayer book. This, too, had been a gift to the new bride. Grisha handled it gently; the worn cover and frayed pages seemed to represent their marriage. Unlike the silver candlesticks, the simple book had no dust on it at all. So she used it regularly, even though she surely knew its contents by heart. He placed it near the wine and went to call his wife to their New Year's table.

Smoothing his tunic, he remembered that his head should be covered. He had no skullcap. Feeling foolish, he put on his NKVD visored cap. He considered turning it around so that the visor pointed backward, but that seemed even more ridiculous. Well, she would understand. He had no choice.

Again he smoothed his tunic and knocked softly on the wardrobe door.

"Rachel Leah, Rachel Leah," he called gently.

Self-consciously, he cleared his throat and knocked again.

"Rachel Leah, may I open the door?" he asked bashfully.

He received no answer.

"I'm opening the door," he announced timidly, as if he were invading the Ark of the Law. He pulled gently on the wardrobe door that covered one-fourth of the front of the massive old cabinet. To his surprise, it was perfectly balanced. Offering no resistance, it swung open easily beneath his touch without even so much as a squeak.

The protective mountain of towels, linens, and tablecloths that mysteriously obscured the interior did not surprise him, but the smell did. He recoiled from the rancid odor of sweat tinged with the bite of dried urine and the slight stench of excrement. He fell back a half step, then held his ground. Breathing through his mouth, he respectfully stepped closer to the amorphous heap of colors and cloths, addressing the Sinai of drapery apologetically as an unworthy supplicant.

"Rachel Leah, your father has written sending his blessings. It is Rosh Hashanah, and I have some—No," he corrected himself, "I was given some kosher wine as a gift. I would like to make kiddush for you."

He stared into the enigmatic folds that veiled the bride of his youth, but he heard nothing, not even the rustle of cloth. One of lesser faith would have wondered whether she truly dwelled inside, but Grisha knew that beneath the layers of years she sat quiet and rejected, imprisoned by his inattention. Grisha did not, however, wonder whether she sat awaiting his call. He had turned away from her; it would be only fair were she to turn away from him.

"Would you like to come out and light the New Year's candles?" he invited gently.

He received no response.

"It has been a very long time," he admitted.

He waited a while and added, "I understand. It has been too long."

Leaving the cupboard door open, Grisha turned to the box of matches. The long wooden sticks crackled into flame with a precision and energy that surprised him. All else in their home seemed so dark, sluggish and weighed down by decades and decay. But the light exploded as if from another world. Grisha remembered something about a match factory in Krimsk. Wasn't there a match factory there? But wasn't Krimsk dark and sluggish? How strangely inappropriate, he thought, but no more so than his lighting the High Holiday candles.

Grisha turned the flaming match to one wick, then the other. The first burned with the steady, even glow that he recalled from his youth, when his mother had waved her arms in silent exhortation, pronouncing the blessing. It was a memory that seemed incredibly distant. He could barely remember Rachel Leah lighting Rosh Hashanah candles at all. Because Grisha felt uncomfortable performing a woman's function, he didn't utter the simple blessing that he knew he could find in the tattered prayer book. He couldn't quite admit this discomfort at taking a woman's role; rather he thought to himself that it would be rude for him to usurp her holy deed in front of her—for he surely felt her presence as if she were seated at the holiday table watching his every motion.

The wick of the second smoke-smeared candle sputtered and seemed to swallow the flame rapaciously. Imperfectly, a thin twisting thread of smoke rose toward the ceiling. It, too, unnerved Grisha, for it seemed to reflect the falseness of his action—even the false state of his soul, although Grisha, of course, didn't believe in any such thing, did he? How could he? He glanced at the high vaulted ceiling, so far above him that he couldn't even detect the black smoke smudging it. That was some consolation, though he knew that if the candle burned long enough, it would surely leave a sooty stain.

Standing alone at his place at the head of the table, he carefully leafed through Rachel Leah's prayer book in search of the blessings that he must recite inaugurating the Day of Judgment. He felt a sense of urgency, for he feared that the frayed edges might crumble in his hands if he continued to cast them about. With relief, he found what he was looking for. The Hebrew text seemed so alien and archaic, with all its little dots and zigzags of vowel sounds swarming above and below and even inside the old-fashioned square letters. Could he still read it? It seemed to call for deciphering more than reading. The first line in large print must be the blessing for wine, one he still knew by heart. The continuation of the blessing of sanctification must certainly begin the same way—"Blessed art Thou, O Lord, King of the Universe." When Grisha saw that indeed it did, he began to develop the confidence that despite all the years, he could probably make it through if he really concentrated.

He opened Svetkov's gift bottle of kosher wine and filled the glass tumbler. The dark wine that had been rushing frantically about in the confining bottle seemed liberated, and it poured forth gracefully into the large glass, where it settled in an open, quiet pool. Grisha felt uncomfortable taking into his hand the heavy drinking glass, larger and more vulgar than the traditional, delicately worked silver cup that he had lost somewhere with the Cossacks. Turning his attention back to the perverse Hebrew alphabet, he found no such immediate repose, for he had to read the recondite markings that he had not been able to flee from in some forlorn Polish town.

Like a young lad in the religious primary school, Grisha stood up, nervously shifting his weight from one foot to the other, as if there were a spot on the floor that would recite the proper words if pressed sufficiently hard. Not finding one, he stood still and squinted at the text in the hope of discerning something that would make everything clear; then realizing that it all depended upon him, Grisha began to read. Uncertain, even stumbling, he recited the familiar blessing over the wine. With increased confidence, he proceeded into the more complex Hebrew of the kiddush, sanctifying the holiday. Concentrating on every letter, he discovered that the strange symbols printed in Rachel Leah's prayer book corresponded to faint tracings in his memory.

He read as if he were merely an instrument of sanctification, surprised and pleased, but not in good conscience able to take credit for a technical feat of memory. As he continued, however, his remembrance became more personal, and he entered into a dialogue with memory. Although he read in a dry, straightforward tone, in his mind he could hear the echo of melodious phrases. Focusing on Rachel Leah's yellowing page for the words to sanctify the Day of Judgment, at the same time he also turned inward to listen to how he had once sung them. At first his interior voice lagged behind. As he approached the end of the paragraph, his memory seemed to catch up, and he chanted the final lines blessing God for sanctifying "Israel and the Day of Remembrance." Grisha was surprised yet comforted to find the New Year, the Day of Judgment, referred to as the Day of Remembrance. Yes, for him it was a day of remembrance. Certainly too late for anything else. Too late for belief, but not too late for remembrance. For that gift he was grateful, and in that spirit he humbly chanted the final holiday blessing, thanking God "for granting us life, for sustaining us, and for permitting us to attain this notable time." Then he seated himself before drinking from the boorish wine goblet.

As he sat down, he thought he heard something, but he was looking down into the dark wine that had released such a flood of memories, as if crushed and fermented from the tight grapes of the mind. Although sure that he had heard it, he was equally sure that it echoed from his dialogue with memory. It was, after all, the Day of Remembrance, so it did not surprise him to hear such a thing. Seated, he leaned toward the full tumbler and raised the glass slightly to his lips. Although he sipped and swallowed the wine, he had no idea how it tasted, for when he began to drink the wine of blessing, he raised his eyes to discover the wife of his youth seated opposite him at the far end of the table. So it was she who had answered, "Amen."

She had emerged in silence. Immersed in sanctifying the Day of Remembrance, he had heard neither the rustle of draperies nor the step of her foot. After losing hope and proceeding alone with everything dependent upon himself, he looked up to find her seated at the table, demure and calm, waiting patiently for her husband to pass her the wine cup. Regret softly touched his heart at having lost the silver goblet—regret at having degraded the kiddush cup, regret at not having regal silvered beauty with which to serve his wife. Rachel Leah's majesty was such that the absence of finery made no difference to her; Grisha felt she deserved such riches all the more.

She sat erect, in quiet dignity. Her garments—the faded cloths of the Mironov mansion—were draped about her in composed, insane elegance. On her head lay three brightly patterned scarves, one not precisely resting upon the other. Under the riot of striped yellow spilled green-and-white checks, and under that escaped a red paisley, swirling upon itself in convolutions darker and richer than wine. She sat erect, her head held high, the pastiche of color adorning her head like the crest of feathers of a tropical bird. But this startling panache was not her most striking feature. Over her shoulder lay draped swaths of curtains—a satin of stark black-and-white stripes crossed her shoulders and plunged down her sides in harsh vertical splendor. The stark black-and-white scarf dominated all. Although it reminded Grisha of a man's prayer shawl, it was much more powerful and arresting in its singularity; draped upon her proud person, it seemed to harken beyond the synagogue back to the majestic rites of temple worship, a veritable priestly vestment.

Ashamed to be serving her in the dull, vulgar brutality of an NKVD uniform, he partially rose from his chair and, remaining slightly stooped to hide his shame, brought her the cup and placed it before her.

She turned to take the glass and turned back to face straight ahead before drinking. Unlike Grisha, she did not lean over, but raised the wine to her lips. Obsequiously observing from afar, Grisha saw something that impressed him. For years he had thought his wife mad; even now he wasn't sure that she wasn't, although he admitted that he and his Soviet Russia were madder than she, and infinitely crueler. Tonight, however, along with the strange distant gleam he knew so well and a deadened look as if her mind were in hibernation along with her body, he saw something radiant and intimate, as if Rachel Leah were responding to the presence of the High Holiday. She was sitting at the table with the Day of Judgment. For a moment Grisha even felt the least bit jealous of the New Year. He felt foolish, but he couldn't help it: she had exhibited such loyalty all these years, and now she exhibited such . . . passion? He wondered whether she might have been hibernating inside the wardrobe for this moment, like a bear sleeping through the winter until springtime. No, that was wrong.

Grisha couldn't think of her as a bear; a bear was much too Russian, too cumbersome, and too plain. Rachel Leah was more like a seed buried underground as if dead, then springing to life in a sudden bloom.

She had finished drinking. Grisha bent forward to remove the glass.

"May you have a good year. May you be inscribed and sealed in the Book of Life on this Day of Judgment," she said to her husband.

Grisha nodded, although he knew how impossible that would be. No God he could imagine could perform such miracles, but for once, he didn't feel sorry for himself. His concern was for Rachel Leah's New Year's banquet.

"All we have is bread. We don't have any honey to dip into for a sweet new year," he confessed.

Rachel Leah nodded. "God will provide," she declared.

Grisha wanted to agree with her, but he found it impossible to imagine just what God could provide in Stalin's Russia. He politely, almost servilely lowered his head, suggesting that he had heard her and that it was neither his wish nor his prerogative to question her judgment. After all, where had his judgment gotten them?

Grisha had returned to his seat when he remembered that religious Jews performed a ritual washing of hands before blessing bread. He went to the sink, filled a cup of water, and poured it over each hand alternately several times. Having finished, he flicked his hands over the sink to drain them of excess water. Then, realizing he would find no towel, he wiped them with abandon on his NKVD tunic and didn't bother to smooth it when he was finished.

He took his place at the head of the table before the

plain loaves. He heard the watery splash of Rachel Leah's ablution and wanted to watch her unobserved as she stood with her back to him, but he restrained himself since he felt that it would be improper. He had coaxed her forth to celebrate the Day of Judgment, and to that he would remain true. Instead Grisha stared intently at the two coarse, dark loaves. According to the traditional manner, he would lift both, pronounce the blessing, and break bread from one of them. But which one? An ordinary Muscovite family was entitled to only one. Grisha's secret police participation had secured them the second. Which was the NKVD loaf? He didn't want to feast on that one. They looked the same, and Grisha knew that "they," the loaves, were the same; they were both NKVD loaves. They had to be; after all, "they" were Grisha himself. His NKVD bread was the only staple he provided. For Rachel Leah they were Rosh Hashanah loaves, so he lifted them off the wooden cutting board. They felt surprisingly light in his hands; their rough crust welcomed his grasp as he blessed God, "who brings forth bread from the earth." Even NKVD bread, he supposed.

"Amen," Rachel Leah responded, "God is a Faithful King."

Grisha put the loaves down, broke off a piece from one, and as soon as he began to chew it, regretted the lack of honey. Not just NKVD bread, all of Russia's poor bread needed to be sweetened. He sat self-consciously eating before his wife, but since he blessed the bread for both of them, the law obliged him to eat first. He quickly swallowed the plain rough bread and broke off another larger piece for Rachel Leah. He rose from his seat and served it to her at the far end of the table. She took it from the plate, extending her hand demurely and not looking at him, and turned away slightly when she took her first bite. She wiped the large crumbs from her lip. She ate slowly, relishing every bite, as if it were the sweetest bread ever baked. Grisha acutely experienced his inadequacy.

"There is no more," he apologized.

She didn't seem to be listening.

"No honey. Nothing else," he commented sadly. He bowed slightly in apology and began to return to his place.

"Wait here," she ordered in a calm, clear voice, but with the unmistakable ring of authority.

Grisha turned back.

"Wait here," she commanded.

"Here?" He pointed to the floor where he was standing, confused as to why he should remain in such an anomalous place when there was nothing more to serve.

"Yes," she insisted without bothering to explain, and continued to eat the piece of blessed bread that he had brought her.

In her hands it didn't seem to be NKVD bread at all, but a loaf worthy of a feast celebrating creation. He waited patiently for the first moments as Rachel Leah calmly continued her ceremonial feasting. Then he began squirming as the time wore on. She savored every particle of her share, concentrating on the simple act of eating with single-minded force. Grisha would not have been surprised had she broken into full-throated song, but he might have been fearful. She seemed to have gathered a power about her that was not to be denied. While breaking the Rosh Hashanah bread, Rachel Leah seemed to possess what Grisha had thought of in the most exuberant days of the Glorious

Revolution as Necessity, something that he had since given up as illusory. Despite his apprehensions, he was curious as to where such a sense of power might lead her, might lead them—for he had become her servant this night, literally waiting on her.

He was calmed by the thought that there really wasn't much Rachel Leah could do with her religious inspiration. Saddened, too; for didn't she deserve an opportunity to express such intense feeling, and wasn't he responsible for her deprivation? It was the Day of Remembrance—for him judgment had already been deservedly decreed, hadn't it? He looked at Rachel Leah's face and remembered the teenage girl that he had married after he had nearly burned to death in saving the Torah scroll from the fire in the Angel of Death synagogue in Krimsk. He recalled the slight, girlish face and, yes, even then it had shone with an ecstasy. That feverish, childish excitement had stimulated young Grisha so deeply that when the rebbe had offered him his daughter, Grisha couldn't refuse. He had wanted to possess her. He, too, was feverish, his fever having been fanned by the flames.

Yes, Grisha remembered her childish enthusiasm. No, it was more than that; Grisha couldn't look into a mirror without becoming ill, but Rachel Leah had stared adoringly at his charred flesh, for he was the man who had saved the Torah. "Let that Torah save you," the rebbe had written, but that seemed beyond reach, impossibly distant, beyond memory. Grisha was pleased at having found the youthful counterpart to the passionate force now in Rachel Leah's face. The face itself was noticeably thirty-three years older, both a victim and a survivor of its fine-boned, almost sharply etched prominence; not her father's smooth skin, nor her mother's fine flesh. Rachel Leah's lack of flesh gave her face a slightly pointy expression that revealed her age but promised to be kinder in the coming decades; her features would retain their shape while other, fuller faces began to decay. Grisha wondered whether Rachel Leah even looked into a mirror anymore; he guessed not. Although curious about her thoughts, he couldn't hazard a guess about them. He did hope that they didn't include him. Not today, the Day of Remembrance, when his remembrances were not flattering; not today, the Day of Judgment, when her judgment of him must certainly be damning.

Distracted by his musings, Grisha now saw that his wife had finished her bread and turned to him, a look of expectation upon her no longer young face.

"Yes?" he asked in polite inquiry.

"Yes," she answered definitively.

"Yes?" he repeated, not understanding at all what Rachel Leah had agreed to.

"Yes," she commanded, sitting regally erect and staring directly at him.

Bewildered, Grisha opened his mouth in the unspoken word "What?" but Rachel Leah didn't answer. Instead, she reached up and removed her yellow scarf. She lifted the riotous yellow stripes from her head and simply let the cloth drop to the floor. Her hand remained at the level of her head, as if she had started to wave to someone, then stopped. Grisha moved to pick up the scarf, but Rachel Leah casually extended her hand, holding her palm upward, fingers upraised. "Leave it," she ordered, and Grisha complied.

He couldn't turn away from the sunburst spread out

limp on the floor, although the green-and-white scarf that now lay fully exposed was not without visual interest. It seemed, however, too obvious in its simple relentless pattern, here green, there white, and again green. When Rachel Leah removed it from her head, letting it fall swiftly to the floor, Grisha was pleased. The rich red paisley that lay beneath it did not disappoint in its revelation. The curves of red spiced with the smaller paramecium-shaped gold, outlined in black, swirled and spiraled about her head like a veritable cloth crown of rubies and wrought gold. Rachel Leah plucked the rich garment from her head as casually as she had the previous two. As it fell softly, she silently rose, standing very straight, as if presiding over the feast table. Her long unkempt hair cascaded about her shoulders in uneven greasy strands of tired brown peppered with listless gray. Their long, wild abundance created the effect of a horse's mane.

Grisha was astonished at the hoary abundance that the precise paisley scarf had liberated. He didn't know whether he was more shocked by the incredible length that had lain hidden or by the torrential amounts of gray that had claimed it—or by what both features implied: the vast amount of time, the many years, in which he had not seen his wife unveiled. He had the impression, although certainly wrong, that he had not seen his wife's hair since their wedding day. Before he could begin to calculate how long it might really have been, she let the strikingly elegant black-and-white stole fall from her shoulders. It fell back, wreathlike, onto her chair, much of it remaining there as long sections slid onto the floor. The cloth had been wound about Rachel Leah and surprised Grisha by its great length. It must have been a curtain from one of the floor-to-ceiling windows of the salon that opened onto the garden. Try as he might, Grisha still could not recall any such distinctive drapery. Before he had a proper chance to calmly reflect on what curtains had been hanging there, he realized that Rachel Leah was continuing to disrobe. A purple sash descended from her bosom and floated onto the pile on the floor. His eyes were drawn to the rich color. His gaze remained on the object at her feet, but from the corner of his eye he saw that some sort of shabby white sweater had been pulled over her head, and then dropped to partially cover the royal purple. Grisha slowly moved forward to raise the purple garment from where it had fallen. With a royal gesture, she restrained him.

Grisha didn't quite grasp what she was doing. It had been so very warm, but he was surprised when her fingers nimbly unbuttoned a faded gray blouse. He turned as she slipped one thin arm out, then the other. Still one step behind her, he caught a glimpse of something ropelike falling away, an expanse of flesh, and then he was dimly aware of Rachel Leah stepping daintily out of a skirt—even several skirts, and then out of undergarments.

Grisha glimpsed an expanse of pale flesh and quickly turned away.

"Yes," Rachel Leah announced firmly.

Confused, Grisha shook his head ever so slightly so that he would not see her.

"Yes," she said again, gently understanding his difficulty. Grisha felt light agile fingers unbuttoning his tunic. Before he could smooth it, it was falling away from him, and then he felt her remove his visored hat.

"No," he protested softly, but her light fingers fluttered

about him until all his garments, NKVD and personal, had fallen in a lifeless heap below.

She reached up and turned his head to face her.

Although he was afraid, he couldn't successfully resist, and she came into his sight.

"Yes," she said, gently insistent.

Fighting an impulse to turn away, he looked at her fearfully. Dmitri Cherbyshev came to mind, and Grisha was afraid that if he did unite with her, blood would gush forth from him, polluting them both in a crimson orgy.

"No!" he said sharply. God, he thought, how he should have shot that disgusting degenerate. But even as he said it, Rachel Leah smiled. Blushing, Grisha looked at the wife of all his adult years. After the sight of her billowing, unkempt gray hair, her body was not a surprise. Pale and slight, her flesh no longer supple, her body sagged, but it did so all in the same direction, downward. For someone who did nothing but sit in a closet, she seemed surprisingly well fed; the slightly drooping flesh softened the wiry angularity of her youth. It was as if her flesh, beginning with her head, had drifted gently downward away from her face, leaving it thin and pointy. Her narrow shoulders were surprisingly straight. Her small, soft drooping breasts were still feminine, but lay as if attached to her pale, sloping stomach. Then Grisha, in spite of himself, looked lower and saw something that amazed him. One aspect of Rachel Leah's appearance had dramatically improved. In her youth her hips and buttocks had been slight, almost boyish, but now the downward flow of flesh had transformed them, gracefully rounding them and giving her the rich, fertile pear shape of womanhood.

"*Babye leto*," he uttered in surprise.

"Yes," she agreed, responding to his aroused state.

She stepped closer to him and began to draw him onto the table.

Although he did not want to contradict her wishes, he found himself protesting in puritanical query, "The bed?" Only ten or twelve feet away, it seemed much more hospitable than the table with the tall candles that burned relentlessly down toward their heavy silver base.

"The Rosh Hashanah table," Rachel Leah proclaimed in exaltation, drawing him onto it and then onto her.

In his timid fear, he lay still, anxious that his feet not knock over her plate and glass or that her hair, spread beneath her like a great speckled heavy mat, not touch the candles. Beneath him he felt Rachel Leah beginning to move her overripe pear-shaped torso in long, slow, comforting undulations. Recalling the Alexandrovsky Gardens, he tried to relax and join Rachel Leah in her celebration of the New Year. Although he desperately wanted to consent to her desires, he lay still, as if paralyzed. Rachel Leah continued her slow, wavelike undulations, which grew stronger and quicker until they gave way to forceful thrusts that flung Grisha about. He, however, still could not respond. Except for his eyes, all parts of his body seemed distant and unattached to his purposeful will. He dreaded desire; not Rachel Leah's, but Dmitri Cherbyshev's and Stalin's with its testicle-crushing spurt of blood. Offended by such impure thoughts, he closed his eyes to drive them from his mind.

Rachel Leah seemed to respond to his closed eyes with increased vigor, and she reinforced her pelvic thrusts with a writhing of her entire body. Grisha clung to her just to keep from falling. He thought he saw a flash of orange-yellow light through his closed eyelids and imagined he heard a crackling sound. Opening his eyes, he gazed at Rachel Leah making love, her head wreathed in a halo of flames.

Grisha lunged forward, pulling the long crackling strands of burning hair from the candles that had ignited them and swiftly beating the flaming crescent crown against the tabletop to extinguish it. He pressed his forearms against the small flames that had begun to lick toward her shoulders, but even as he did so, his already scorched hands were smoothly and surely caressing the fiery halo nearer her head, suffocating the fire against the still unburnt hair nearest her scalp. With small patting gestures he stifled the flames before flying onto the next smoldering patch. Only when he was certain that she was in no danger of immolation did he stop his frenzied cupping of her head and turn more calmly to pat some of the longer ringlets that still glowed with the potential to rekindle the fearful flames. For good measure, closing his hands in a half-fist, he pushed away the two great silver candlesticks. He then slid back to face her. Rachel Leah's expression of divine ecstasy had not lessened. He wondered whether she was even aware that she had almost burned to death.

"Are you all right?" he asked gently.

In answer, she guided him back inside her. Amid the horrible, almost suffocating stench of burned human hair, he successfully culminated the physical act—gently mourning their lives while softly celebrating their union.

CHAPTER TWELVE

Minutes later, as he lay next to her, the pain of his burned hands ground through him in a stream of pulsating agony. The flames had even singed his eyebrows, shrinking and frizzling them into hard little wires. He recalled the day in the Angel of Death so long ago when he had saved the Torah, and emerged in ashes to be awarded Rachel Leah.

"The Day of Remembrance. Nothing has changed," he said to himself and to Rachel Leah.

"Something has," she insisted.

"We must elevate the royal purple garment that lies on the floor," he said.

"We already have," she informed him.

He turned to her with a questioning look.

"I'm pregnant," she announced with quiet certainty.

Grisha feared that she believed it, poor thing. He wondered why she had continued to lie uncovered. He had offered her the purple sash, but she had refused, explaining that it was as hot as fire in the room. He knew all about that. Indeed, with the pain in his hands, he would ask her to dress him. That was only fair; after all, she had undressed him. But pregnant? After all these years? Poor Rachel Leah was mad. Well, she came by that legitimately from her father, the Krimsker Rebbe. Yes, he must remind her to read her father's letter. Suddenly Grisha thought that maybe she had. No, she couldn't have. Perhaps she didn't need to, since she was the rebbe's daughter. She already knew the secret of Rosh Hashanah: creation. That must be why she thought she was pregnant. Grisha would have to ask her what the rebbe meant about his being "not too old to fly." Most of the other things he understood, even if he didn't believe them.

He turned to ask what the rebbe meant about learning to fly, leather jackets, and scarves, but he saw Rachel Leah lying next to him. Her face was at the center of a shell of twisted, scorched hair the color of ash. The ends of the once long mane that had burned away were indeed a light gray. In the midst of such destruction—a hairbreadth from disaster—Rachel Leah's face was perfectly serene. How long had it been since he had seen her like that? Had he ever? He couldn't disturb her, but she was the rebbe's daughter, and Grisha was sure that she knew what the letter meant. Well, if Grisha wasn't quite serene himself, he was exhausted and in pain, and he had had more than enough insights for one day. Enough for a lifetime, and he could face Lenin and Stalin, which was only fair, for ultimately "they" were he. He, however, was even worse, because he himself had debased the King's porphyra, the royal purple garment that is Israel and God's glory. But now in some sense he was more than "they," for he had recaptured a little of Rosh Hashanah.

He leaned over and kissed Rachel Leah's hand. She responded by gently tracing her finger across his cheek, smoothly and tranquilly. He lay quietly so as not to disturb her. So he would never learn to fly.

She lay quietly so as not to disturb their child.

CHAPTER THIRTEEN

WHEN THEY CAME FOR HIM THAT NIGHT, THEY KNOCKED on the upstairs door just the way they were supposed to. There were four of them. Orlov was not among them, although he might have been, since they were all "new men," correct and efficient. They asked him to identify himself; they requested his pistol; they told him to follow them. For his part, Grisha complied fully, but he couldn't muster the defiance of a Sergei Gasparov or summon the submissiveness of a Dmitri Cherbyshev. Stolid and dull, he had lost the grace of his earlier insights. Led down the grand staircase, out of Mironov's mansion, and into the impenetrable darkness of a black Fiat, he was simply fearful. Fearful of suffering, fearful of dying. He felt very small and incapable of bravery, despite the dull awareness that his burned hands ached and that his most sensitive flesh stuck painfully to his pants as if glued with honey.

He felt too old to fly, which was a tragic shame; that might have been the only way to escape when the bullet tore into the back of his head in the basement of the Lubyanka.

AIR WAVES

IN SPITE OF A SEVERE HEADACHE THAT HAD SUDDENLY attacked the rebbe on Rosh Hashanah eve, 1936, and plagued him for nine whole months, the rebbe continuously scanned the skies for unidentified aircraft. A powerful intimation of unknown planes suddenly appearing in American Hawaii had begun to haunt him; and he vaguely sensed a danger from the Far East. Nor did he discount the more benign possibility that his son-in-law, Hershel, would have to escape to St. Louis by an Asian-Pacific route; therefore the rebbe peered anxiously and expectantly into both the western and eastern skies. This swiveling of his aching head, necessary for patrolling two horizons, proved excruciatingly painful. Shayna Basya, his rebbetzin, could not get him inside the house. As winter approached, she feared for her husband's health and yearned for the days back in Krimsk when he had disappeared into his study. With the help of Sammy Rudman, son of Boruch Levi Rudman from Krimsk, she convinced the rebbe to transfer his private air patrol from the street onto their large second-floor balcony, which opened off the kitchen.

From inside the door the rebbetzin kept him supplied with blankets and hot thermos bottles of coffee. At sundown, complaining of a headache but never of the cold, he would stagger inside and collapse onto his bed. During this period he did not descend below the second floor, and therefore he effectively disappeared from the beis midrash and the life of St. Louis, if not from view (the balcony overlooked the street). He even lost interest in the American Indian. When F.D.R. wanted to appoint the rebbe to a national Indian commission in Washington, D.C., the rebbe evinced no interest whatsoever. When Yitzhak Weinbach sent his son-in-law, Sammy Rudman, onto the air patrol balcony to try to convince the rebbe to accept the honor, the rebbe momentarily lowered his gaze from the skies and said, "If Reb Zelig were still alive, I think I would have him say kaddish for General Custer and remove Tsar Nicholas II from his list." Sammy understood that the rebbe's attitude had changed. He reported back to his father-in-law that the rebbe feared that too much Jewish interest in the Indian question might raise the charge of dual loyalties. Sammy's reform Jewish father-in-law readily accepted the rebbe's demurral and congratulated Sammy on his spiritual mentor's political acumen. For Hanukkah, Yitzhak Weinbach sent the rebbe a dozen pairs of all-wool stockings.

The rebbetzin accepted the gift, thinking that a mere dozen pairs would prove insufficient to see the rebbe through his "heavenly exile"—for that was how she and the Jewish community referred to it—but she was wrong. Although the heavenly vigil continued throughout the winter, one night in the late spring, the rebbe woke the rebbetzin.

"Do you hear crying? A baby crying?" he asked.

"No," she answered. "Why?"

"It certainly sounds like our grandchild, but it's probably just the holy Shekinah crying in the impure diaspora," he murmured, and rolled over and went back to sleep.

The rebbetzin listened carefully, but heard nothing. She could not fall asleep for some time. When she awoke in the morning, it was already late. She rushed into the kitchen to make coffee for her husband, who by now must have been searching the skies for several hours. She put up the porcelain coffeepot and hurried to the balcony to apologize for having overslept. Not seeing him, she had opened the door to go outside when she heard a voice behind her.

"Close the door, please. That creates a terrible draft," the rebbe said.

She turned around to find the rebbe seated at the kitchen table, leisurely reading the morning paper.

"What are you doing here?" she asked in surprise.

"Reading the paper. I'll be finished with it in a minute. Do you mind?" he asked solicitously.

"Oh, no."

"Please, the draft," he reminded her.

"Yes, sorry," she said, and closed the door.

When she served him his coffee, she couldn't help blinking her eyes to be sure that he really was perusing the newspaper at the table and not scanning the skies from the porch.

"Anything new?" she asked searchingly.

"Nothing very good," he replied, exchanging the paper for his coffee.

"You're not going outside today?" she asked tentatively.

"No, if you want to use the balcony, go right ahead. In this sunny spring weather, it's really very pleasant."

The rebbetzin nodded.

"You'll enjoy it," he said. "Excuse me, I have work to do," he added, taking his coffee and going into his study.

The rebbetzin glanced down at the headlines. Hitler, that horrendous German anti-Semite, was featured prominently in them, but she didn't think the newspaper had anything to do with the rebbe's ending his vigil. The business about a baby, much less a grandchild, crying in the night seemed more relevant, but that didn't make any sense either. In fact, the one thing she was sure of was that she really didn't know what to think. No, she was sure of one other thing. The rebbe had ended his heavenly exile.

She walked over to the door and went out onto the lonely balcony. The rebbe was right; it really was very pleasant in the spring sunshine. Without thinking, she began to imitate the rebbe and looked about the sky as if she were a member of the civil air patrol. As awkward as she felt, she knew that she certainly wasn't a participant in the heavenly exile. Still, she wondered whose crying baby had awakened the rebbe.

The rebbe returned to his beis midrash and a more normal life for the remainder of the decade, but even the rebbe wasn't completely impervious to time. During the winter spent exposed to the elements he had grown older, although from his appearance alone, one could not guess his age. He was aging, all right, but as he did so, the smooth skin simply stretched tighter across the strong facial bones, preventing any wrinkles from forming, even though it was plain that the skin itself was not fleshy and vibrant like that of a younger man. He was aging, but very slowly, and in a manner that suggested preservation more than deterioration, like a gourd. His hair and beard were no longer as dark as they once had been. Here and there were areas that might be described as no longer black, but rather the dull shade of very dark ash. The most pronounced sign of age, however, was that the Krimsker Rebbe just did not move so quickly. One could no longer imagine him scrambling onto the roof of an automobile to deliver a eulogy, as he once had.

After Hitler invaded Poland, everyone everywhere, including in the beis midrash, was talking about the fate of Jews in occupied Poland and especially in Krimsk, but when the rebbe entered for the evening service, everyone quieted down. That is, everyone except for one congregant. The young American came forward and announced that now, in the light of the latest events in the old country and in Poland, in particular—for now Krimsk had fallen under Hitler's rule—it was clear how smart the rebbe had been in getting the Jews out of there and in bringing them to America. "An act of genius, bringing the Jews to the blessed land of America," he declared. "Why, we should dance on the tables from joy!"

The rebbe, who had taken his seat on the eastern wall behind his table upon which the young enthusiast proposed to dance, looked up with a frown.

"Stay off the tables; they are holy!" he ordered.

The rebbe turned to Sammy and said, "America is blessed. Here idiots don't have to run around with their mouths open; they can even become president." The rebbe was referring to Warren Harding. For reasons Sammy had never understood, the rebbe had never gotten over his disappointment in Presidents Harding and Coolidge.

Sammy often understood the rebbe's cryptic remarks; what the rebbe didn't say often left him uncertain. What Sammy was wondering now was, if America did get involved in the war, might the prediction the rebbe had once made about him come true: would be become a pilot? Suddenly the rebbe glanced at him and advised, "Stay out of airplanes. You're married."

In 1941, when America did enter the war and civil air patrols were formed, the city remembered the rebbe's peerless vigil and turned to him for advice about training and winter observation, but by then he was unavailable. The rebbe had entered his study and was not to be disturbed.

II
THE
STRENGTH
OF STONES

If stones fall on a clay cooking pot, woe unto the pot; if the pot falls on stones, woe unto the pot. In any event, it is woe unto the pot.

—Midrash Esther Rabba

WARSAW
1942

YOM KIPPUR
(THE DAY OF ATONEMENT)

On Yom Kippur, the Day of Atonement, it is forbidden to eat or to drink.

Accompanied by penitence, either death or Yom Kippur atones for sin.

Yom Kippur atones for sins between man and God.
Yom Kippur does not atone for sins between man and his fellow until one has placated his fellow.

—The Mishnah, Tractate Yoma

If it were not for Yom Kippur, the Day of Atonement, the world could not exist, for Yom Kippur atones both in this world and in the world to come. Sometime in the future when all other festivals and holy days disappear, Yom Kippur will remain.

—Pirkei Rabbi Eliezer

DEFINITIONS AND FINDINGS

IN RESPONSE TO THE CHALLENGE OF MODERNITY, THE Bund suggested that Jews should be socialists who lived their modern socialist Jewish lives speaking Yiddish in Europe. It wasn't always easy to define the Bund, just as it wasn't always easy for them to define themselves, and many people had serious doubts about them. The universalist Marxists found them parochial, the labor Zionists found them in Europe instead of Palestine, the traditional religious Jews found them in violation of Jewish law, the halacha. One political entity harbored no doubts but did have a single criticism: Hitler found them alive.

THE GHETTO

Only misery and Jews were in abundance in the Warsaw ghetto. As the misery increased, the Jews declined; by July 1942 over 100,000 of the ghetto's inhabitants had died within its walls. In the same month, July, the Nazis began mass deportations, which lasted until early September. Special transport trains removed an average of 5,000 to 7,000 Jews each day, for a total of over 300,000.

After a pause of little more than a week, an additional 2,000 Jews gathered for deportation. Like the others in the great deportation, they were told that they were leaving the Warsaw ghetto for "resettlement in the East." Like the others, they, too, marched to the ghetto's railhead at Dzika and Stawki Streets. Unlike the others, however, they assembled on the holiest day of the Jewish year, Yom Kippur, the Day of Atonement.

CHAPTER FOURTEEN

DZIKA AND STAWKI STREETS. MORE THAN HALF THE Warsaw ghetto had already been liquidated, but at Dzika and Stawki Streets Jews still gathered by the thousands. The captive Jews milled about a large enclosure surrounded by barbed wire, armed sentries, and guard dogs. At the *umschlagplatz,* the gathering point, the former residents of the Warsaw ghetto waited to board a train for "resettlement in the East."

DZIKA AND STAWKI STREETS. HE, TOO, WAS WAITING for the train. He knew and he didn't know, and he couldn't remember his name. He knew and he didn't know, and he couldn't remember his name. He was waiting for the train. He knew and he didn't know—and he didn't care. He couldn't remember his name—and about that he did care. He was waiting for the train, and the train would certainly arrive because it was a Nazi train, a Nazi locomotive of energy and force. What about his name? It must be a Jewish name, no?

CHAPTER FIFTEEN

DZIKA AND STAWKI STREETS. HE WASN'T ALONE. Thousands waited, he among them, like a . . . ? Like a . . . ? He was tempted to say, "Like a sea of humanity," but that wasn't quite right. They weren't numerous enough to be a sea. The Germans and their helpers were the sea. The Jews of Warsaw were drowning in a sea of inhumanity that was Europe. So who were they, these sinking Jews who had gathered at Dzika and Stawki Streets? If Europe was the sea, then were the Jews an island about to be reclaimed by the primitive ocean that had once covered all the land? The Jews had "surfaced" in Europe, and they were being submerged, but a drowned land becomes part of the vast sea floor until some future time, when it may reappear. The Nazis, however, were destroying the Jews without trace, unlike the deep, murky seabed that still remains an essential part of the planet with all its contours intact, however pressed by salty water and the brittle clambering feet of crustaceans. Although Atlantis might have been buried beneath the waves, the great wide sea also bespoke nurture— deep, silent, and chilled, where life had originally formed.

Poland had become a boundless cemetery of unmarked, unattended graves. What nurture did a grave offer? Nothing to the one who escaped into nonbeing; yet his body would compliantly rot to fertilize fields of grain that would feed the savages of the Third Reich, all in accordance, no doubt, with some physical law of nutrients that had already been charted on an SS office wall in Berlin.

The Jews would be consumed aboveground and belowground, time and time again. There was no escape, only surrender. Shamefully, he was prepared to surrender. He would welcome the loss of pain, the loss of awareness that meant being a Jew aboveground in the Third Reich. So why did he need a name?

Dzika and Stawki Streets. Everyone knew, and no one knew.

In this, at least—whatever his name was—he was like everyone else. The Nazis claimed they were shipping the Jews for "resettlement in the East," but everyone knew the Nazis were shipping them to their deaths. What possible use could the Nazis have for Jews? The Germans had robbed them, beaten them, uprooted them, herded them into a squalid barbed wire ghetto where they continued to beat, murder, and degrade them. Jews were compared to tubercle bacilli, and what did civilized people do with germs in the twentieth century? Obviously they identified them, isolated them, and destroyed them. The Germans had already identified the Jews with yellow stars that said "Jude," and the Germans had already isolated them in a tightly sealed ghetto marked by signs declaring, "Danger, Epidemic Zone." What else remained? Only "resettlement in the East"! Indeed, Jewish messengers from Chelmno had reached the ghetto in Warsaw and revealed that the Nazis were systematically gassing the Jews in special killing vans. It was rumored that recently Jews had discovered the destination of the trains—Treblinka, after which all traces of the passengers were lost.

Still they gathered at Dzika and Stawki Streets. What choice did they have? To fight? The British, Russian, French, and American armies couldn't defeat the Germans. Could the naked, starving Jews of the Warsaw ghetto, right in the middle of the Nazi empire? Who at the *umschlagplatz* could not know what "resettlement in the East" really meant? Everyone knew. The Nazis, the Jews, the guard dogs, the barbed wire, the cattle cars, the hot, murky sky, the half-empty ghetto, and above all the unrelenting steel rails that led across the horizon into the East. Everyone and everything knew.

Resettlement in the East? What could that mean? Of course no one knew! At least no one at Stawki and Dzika Streets knew! How could they have known? After the hunger, the starvation, the freezing deprivation of the winter, the bestial terror of the summer—the Germans shot "unauthorized" Jews on sight—who could imagine a worse fate? The filth, the overcrowding, the stench of overtaxed sanitary facilities, the reek of sewage, the rumbling carts stacked with corpses—after centuries not only had the ghetto returned, but with it the plague! Who could imagine a worse fate? Not the Jews from the ghetto.

What about the reports from Chelmno: gassing Jews in vans? Who could believe such a mad story? Everyone knew they were out of their minds. More recently, the stories of trainloads disappearing in a place called Treblinka. The whole thing was unbelievable, and wasn't the ghetto constantly swarming with the most bizarre rumors, both morbid and wistful? If one could eat rumors, the ghetto could feed all of Poland! And if there were some Jews killed in Chelmno, weren't they in the East, and hadn't they been helping the Bolsheviks fight the Germans? Wasn't there a war? And when it came to killing, Poles had been murdered, too, and in sizable numbers. It wasn't just the Jews. Since the Germans couldn't exterminate everyone, the rumors of genocide simply couldn't be true.

Such hysterical tales defied logic. If the Germans wanted to kill the Jews of Warsaw, why would they bother to ship them anywhere? They could do it right here. What could stop them? Nothing, so the Nazis must be shipping them somewhere for a purpose. Involved in a massive war, the Germans needed workers. What master would kill his own slaves? Even evil pharaoh didn't do such a thing! Pharaoh afflicted them, but he didn't kill them. He needed them, and so did Hitler. The Jews weren't fooled. They knew Hitler would continue to afflict them in the East. Resettlement wouldn't be easy, but the Jews had outlived pharaoh and a host of other tormentors, and they would outlive Hitler, too—in the East or wherever else he chose to send them.

No, no one knew what "resettlement in the East" really was. No one had been there. That was the logic of the matter. What else could one rely on in an illogical world? Luck? The Jews didn't have any. Faith? That was relevant for some and for their god, perhaps, but it didn't seem capable of affecting the Germans, at least not in this world. So there was only logic, and no one knew. Still, everyone with any sense was afraid. It wasn't always a blessing to have sense; you could choke on the fear—but you couldn't eat it!

CHAPTER SIXTEEN

EVERYONE WAS AFRAID TO BE LEAVING THE GHETTO.
Well, almost everyone. He wasn't afraid. He was relieved,
and that was his sin, the worst of all. The others' fear demonstrated their desire to live. His apathy testified that the
Nazis had won. What would Zigelboym say?

What if someone asked him who he was? What would
he say? What lie could he tell? It would have to be a lie,
wouldn't it? He was ashamed of himself. Indeed, there
wasn't very much to be proud of at Dzika and Stawki
Streets. He was proud of Zigelboym, only of Shmuel Zigelboym, also known in the Bund as Comrade Artur. Only
Zigelboym had not cooperated, and only he had escaped.
A year ago, when the Nazis had called for the Jews to enter
the ghetto, he insisted that they not cooperate in such an
absurd and evil undertaking. Shmuel Mordechai Zigelboym—Comrade Artur! A man like that had two names;
a man like that deserved two names!

If someone asked him who he was, could he use Zigelboym's name? No, that would violate Shmuel's courage, his foresight, his success. Perhaps he could say, "I am Zigelboym's brother!" No, a true brother would have followed Zigelboym in refusing to cooperate with the Nazis in such futile self-degradation, and he had not. No one had, but the Nazis refused to believe it, and they accused Zigelboym of heading an underground organization. The Gestapo wanted to liquidate him, and the Bund insisted that he flee. Only Zigelboym had escaped to London because he refused to cooperate with evil. Now it was too late; the Jews had been herded into the trap. Now civil disobedience would be pointless, silent suicide, and no hindrance to the Nazis. Yes, he knew that now. Now that it was too late. Yes, he was Zigelboym's brother—Zigelboym's idiot brother. Let the idiot remain silent. Perhaps he would smile. Yes, he would smile shamefully and stupidly. That would be no lie. But at Dzika and Stawki Streets it was hard to smile, however stupidly, however shamefully. Zigelboym had not remained silent, but his idiot brother had no choice.

CHAPTER SEVENTEEN

AND SO IT WAS AT DZIKA AND STAWKI STREETS.

A man approached with an inquiring look: You are? Are you?—Yes, he encouraged, I am . . . ?—No, a head shake. No, sorry, you're not . . . ?

No, I suppose not. He would have known. I should know. I am . . . but I don't remember. No longer an "I," he didn't remember.

A woman nodded. They had been neighbors in the ghetto. She lived in the building across the way, but they didn't know one another's names. They had barely spoken. He nodded and smiled at her in a pleasant, almost inviting manner. Altogether inappropriately, altogether idiotically, as if they were starting out on an excursion to the country and he was suggesting that they sit together in the touring coach. The woman's eyes barely flickered in acknowledgment. She responded in accordance with the endless barbed wire, the rigid guns pointing at them, the dignified, well-fed dogs strolling along the perimeter, and the dilapidated cattle cars that sat waiting for them. She was right, and he

[1 6 8]

was wrong. He was an idiot. And that was one more reason to get it all over with.

But he was ashamed because he couldn't remember his name. He was only "he." He couldn't remember his name, and therefore he couldn't say "I." He couldn't say "I was born in Krimsk." He couldn't say, "I am a Jew," because he didn't know who the "I" was. No, he was only "he," because unlike an "I," a "he" could be anonymous. So unknown to himself, he waited at Dzika and Stawki Streets because he was a Jew. In his case the Nazis were right to laugh derisively at the stupid Jew. What could be more stupid than forgetting one's name? He would be better off if he were a real idiot and not some overbright fool. Indeed, he would be better off if he were dead. So what? What did he care? The Nazis had long ago taught Jews to say with perfect belief, "I am going to die." It was absolutely nothing to say, "He is going to die." One could say that with complete ease. Where else in the Warsaw ghetto could one find such ease? "He" had a lot to be thankful for, even with the attendant shame, didn't he?

And a lot to be ashamed of, too.

CHAPTER EIGHTEEN

ONLY ZIGELBOYM HAD SURVIVED. ALL THE OTHERS had been overwhelmed. Zigelboym had understood, and only Zigelboym was safe. In the midst of the dark, barbarous Nazi swamp called Europe, there was a single just fact: Zigelboym was safe. In London. It wasn't enough to give anyone else hope, but it was a pleasing thought. A memento of a civilized world one could barely remember. At Dzika and Stawki Streets, the Nazis ruled with unchallenged fury. Universal fury. If it weren't for Zigelboym, a world without Nazis could not be imagined. Only because of Shmuel Zigelboym did London exist. Only because of Zigelboym did the Allies struggle, however lamely, however distantly. He couldn't quite picture Shmuel Zigelboym safe in London. He could see him standing quietly, composed and safe, but he couldn't really picture London. Zigelboym seemed to be a real figure floating in an illusory shimmering haze. That's all London was, a shimmering bright haze. After all, how real could a world without Nazis be?

He smiled ruefully. It was a good thing he didn't believe in an afterlife, because if he did, heaven would have to be populated with Nazis, too. A sad fate for heaven. God, their captive, would sit in judgment in the celestial assembly, the heavenly Judenrat. And God could do no better than commit suicide just as Adam Czernikow had, the head of the Warsaw ghetto Judenrat. That was a few months ago in July, when Czernikow realized the true state of affairs and his own role in them. Well, God could do worse than to imitate Adam Czernikow. The head of the Judenrat didn't fool the Nazis. No one could, but still, you had to admire Czernikow's energy in killing himself. "Energy" was a Nazi property. The Nazis possessed energy. The Nazis possessed all the energy.

CHAPTER NINETEEN

AND TODAY WAS YOM KIPPUR. AT DZIKA AND STAWKI Streets, Jews were praying furtively. As he watched them praying, he could generate no affection, not even any respect, for their action. Nonsense, he thought, simple nonsense. So this was Yom Kippur, the holiest day of the Jewish year. The Day of Atonement, when, they believed, their fate was sealed. Didn't they realize their fate had been sealed long ago—in Berlin—in the Reichstag, when Hitler had come to power? Fate sealed, the only atonement possible: God must atone to man, and since He is as defenseless against Germans as the Jews are, a lot of good that would do.

Although he himself didn't believe in God, he felt sorry for God; it was a difficult time for anything Jewish, even a Jewish God. Even Jews were heard to slander Him and accuse Him of being a Nazi. On that count, he felt sorry for the mythical folk concept. So if God weren't omniscient, omnipotent, and all-merciful, it didn't make Him a Nazi. It might make Him a rather ineffective deity, even a divine failure, but hardly a Nazi.

Not that he believed in such things; still, he thought about Him. After all, He was the Holy One that he had grown up with, the God of his youth, some folkloristic baggage he was destined to drag around all his days like some traveler who was forever walking out the door with an empty suitcase. But there is a certain comfort in traveling with a suitcase, even an empty one. It more than fills the hand; why, with its rigid angles, straight lines, and voluminous bulk, it can fill one's life with security and a sense of order. A man of property, a man of plans. A man with a suitcase looks like someone. What was in his suitcase?—The God of his fathers. Even without belief, it was surprising how often he reflected on the relevance of the God of his fathers to any given situation: what would He think? Why might He have done that? What does He feel? But after all, what did it really matter? It was an imaginary suitcase, and his alone at that. What was real? He knew what was real, all right. The one whose existence no one questioned was the porter who was turning them all into excess baggage, the Angel of Death.

He watched them; furtively huddled together, they fought the Angel of Death through prayer. With no faith in prayer, but with unbounded respect for the Angel of Death, he broke off a small crumb of bread from the stale hunk in his pocket and brought it into the air. Before he could begin to nibble, a fly landed on it. Hitler must have trained the insect personally, he thought. The fly crawled greedily over the morsel, exploring its stale beauty. If not a Nazi party member, the fly was certainly worthy of their respect, sharing the führer's lust for Jews going hungry. He managed to brush the insect away and put the small crumb into his mouth, cradling it under his famished tongue. His touch was less energetic but every bit as passionate as the fly's had been. And they had another thing in common. Neither recognized the fast of Yom Kippur.

CHAPTER TWENTY

THE NAZIS HAD THE ENERGY. THE JEWS HAD FEAR—
and a few crusts of bread.

Afraid that she might be attacked and robbed of her
offspring, a mother held her child close to her the way
he and others clung to their dry crusts of bread, with an
animal passion, ready to die for it if necessary, and with a
tender sensual thrill at touching one's beloved object with
one's very own fingers. With many having already been
shipped away, children were rare as bread in the ghetto.
The mother, though, would suffer all the more. The bread
could be eaten; what could she do with the child? He
had no children and would avoid such suffering. Thank
God for that.

And those who clung to God, they, too, were gathered
at the *umschlagplatz*. Afraid lest the Ukrainian auxiliaries
beat them with their rifle butts or turn their dogs loose
upon them, they furtively prayed under the leaden Polish
sky. Hiding their faces, they barely glanced at one another,

carefully timing their shuffling so as not to appear synchronized. They prayed to a God who had hidden His face from them. Certain in their own faith, they would suffer all the more; for their own pain, and far worse for the pain and suffering they were causing His name.

Since he had left God in his boyhood town of Krimsk, he had been spared that anguish. It seemed good fortune to have turned his back on God before God could turn His divine back on him. Unlike God, *he* hadn't turned his back on his own people. He had written cultural features for Bund publications, and if he had been a lukewarm local Jewish socialist, it was because he felt that the Bund was too doctrinaire and parochial. There was after all something in the tradition besides clericalism, and as impractical and utopian as Zionism was for three million Polish Jews, it wasn't simply a chauvinist tool of capitalism.

No, even if he couldn't quite define what the "Jewish soul" was, he knew it existed, and it was too complex and too sensitive to be reduced to a party platform, no matter how well meaning. He might not have been the theoretician they had expected him to be, but he had never been anything less than faithful to the Jewish soul. At least until recently, when everything just wore him down until he no longer seemed to care. And in fact he really didn't care enough to be angry with God. Not that he believed in the traditional, personal, omnipotent deity. So far as he believed—and it wasn't very far—he opted for Spinoza's god, who had created the laws of nature and did not control individual destinies. But now he no longer much cared about anyone's god, Spinoza's or anyone else's. Still, he remembered God's name; he wished that he could remember his own. Why should he be more solicitous of an ancient god than of himself? He wondered with an irony that lacked sufficient passion for any really tasty bitterness. He would abandon everyone just as God had; instead, he turned to the steel rails—parallel, precise, enduring, and leading away from the Warsaw ghetto.

CHAPTER TWENTY-ONE

DZIKA AND STAWKI STREETS. OTHERS FEARED THE *umschlagplatz,* but it was all right with him. He was going to meet the train. Like the parallel metal bands of track that connected the distant horizons, trains seemed to run through the great moments of his life, from the station at Sufnitz to the *umschlagplatz* here in the Warsaw ghetto.

And he met the train.

The German hosts herded their parasitic guests through a gate in the barbed wire to an adjacent compound and from there into the cattle cars. Having overstayed their welcome, the guests did not resist; indeed, rather apologetically they accepted their hosts' impatient directives to terminate their loitering at Dzika and Stawki Streets. Even after the carriages were full, they assented to their hosts' insistent wish that they continue to enter. For their part, to communicate their seriousness, the hosts shoved, beat, and kicked them. Considering the duration of the guests' stay, a millennium give or take a century, their forced removal went very well.

CHAPTER TWENTY-TWO

UNLIKE THE OTHERS INSIDE THE CATTLE CAR, HE HAD all the air he needed. Still, he could not breathe because everyone else was behind him, pressing pitilessly against his back, which in turn painfully crushed his chest against the slats.

Outside—on the far side of the ghetto—he could distinctly hear the guard dogs barking. Raucous and agitated, they hoarsely trumpeted the frustration of abandoning the hunt. The turbulent stampeding merriment of loading the prey had cruelly stimulated their instinctual desires. They were of good stock, well-bred, finely disciplined, and their clamor demonstrated the primitive vigor of their purpose.

Inside, he envied their deep-throated, full-lunged call, almost Wagnerian in its bold, robust spirit. He wondered whether there would be such performances at the destination in the East. The German shepherds seemed so deeply representative of the West he was leaving that it was hard to imagine them in the East. One had to admire their tireless efficiency. Could the East produce such spirited wonders?

Before he could begin to imagine an answer, a high-pitched voice inside the train car began to howl in a wild instinctual shriek of sustained pain. From his stay in the ghetto, he knew that such cries of terror were raised in pitch, so that one could not discern whether the source was a man or woman. In the small confines of the car the sound reverberated with the fierceness of a siren. Despite the pain it caused the ear, it generated very little opposition, for it gave voice to the others' suffering. Moreover, the residents of the Warsaw ghetto had experienced enough suffering to understand that nothing could be done about such a shriek from the depths of one's being—or as the religious would have it, from the soul when it was leaving the body. He did not admire the energy of the scream; he, too, recognized it as a final sound announcing the death of an organism, like the flash of the flickering wick before its abrupt dark death. He passively listened instead to the will to live draining from a body. It continued for an astonishingly long time. So long, in fact, that it seemed to voice more than the suffering of the one cattle car of the one train. It seemed to articulate the death of the Jewish world itself, as if, he thought, the vault of the sky were a baby's behind and the skin was being stripped off with brutal precision.

A few years ago, even one year ago, he was certain that such a cry would be heard from one end of the world to the other; now he knew that it was muffled by a few score bodies inside the decrepit cattle car, and that outside, the barking of the guard dogs rendered it unintelligible. He couldn't be upset about that; even he preferred the beasts' ravenous call to this lamentable wail; they had the creative energy of the hunt. At least Western dogs moved forward.

All the East did was wail into the grave. And he didn't even have enough spirit to do that while the dome of the Jewish heaven was flayed alive. Did Zigelboym know?

As the screaming cry diminished, he identified the voice as that of a woman. The shriek started to rise again, only to tail off abruptly into sobs of no great distinction.

Almost as an afterthought, someone bothered to explain, "It's for her child."

Another disembodied voice, equally weary, from somewhere behind him in the car asked rhetorically, "They took him from her?"

"No," came the equally logical reply of one facing resettlement in the East. "Because he's still with her. She couldn't leave him behind."

Silence in the car. He welcomed the uninterrupted barking of the dogs. It was so blissfully unambiguous.

CHAPTER TWENTY-THREE

The day wore on. He stood, stuffed bestially into the cattle car. No, not even beasts were shipped to slaughter like this; they would die on their journey and lose their market value. But a Jew had no market value, so in the car they crushed one another: elbows, knees, heads, piercing another's calves, backs, stomachs, sides, every man and child receiving, transmitting, radiating pain, like raindrops striking a pond. Agonies of discomfort crossed the car, reaching those packed against the sides of the carriage. Like a true wave striking a barrier, the pain fell back on itself recrossing the pool. Those mashed against the wall—he was one of them—were the boundary. Although they could originate pain, they could only transmit in one direction. Of these marginal people they were quite literally the most marginal, not fully resonating to their fellows' suffering. On the other hand, they had more air to breathe, and during daylight hours they might even manage a few rays of sunlight, provided of course they weren't crushed to death while enjoying their marginal benefits. The slatted sides built to house Polish cattle and swine were even less relenting than the bony jaws, pointed limbs, and other anatomical instruments of group torture.

What could a Jew lose in this situation that he had not lost already? His life? But it had no market value! What was left? What should have been left? Only the dignity of his name, and he himself had forgotten that. He felt as if he were collaborating with the Nazis. They were bad enough, one didn't have to help them. He had been forgetting his name more and more frequently, for longer and longer periods. Now he seemed to have forgotten it altogether. He had slight hope of remembering; he had begun dreaming of his boyhood town, Krimsk. At first he had assumed that he was subconsciously associating the hunger of Warsaw's ghetto with the deprivation of his youth, as if in some way the stomach sat on memory. He had assumed that a full stomach smothered memory, suppressing its activity.

He had naively thought that the emptiness of his stomach would be compensated for by the fullness of memory, but it was more complex than that. And wasn't he a great one for discovering complexities! For reveling in them! His hunger seemed to stimulate sense areas of his memory and simultaneously to repress others—what was his name!

At night he dreamed of the small leather shop in Krimsk. He could even smell the cracked leather harnesses, the dark sticky glue. A father, a mother, a brother, a sister, called him by name in the night. By day they became pale shadows, mute flickering images, and he could not remember his name. When he squinted to catch the name printed on the shop's door, all he could make out was the fretwork of his own eyelashes, and fuzzily at that. He didn't remember his name.

Indeed, he had thought of taking advantage of those periods when he did know his name to sew it into his coat or write it on a piece of paper to be carried in his pants pocket, but that would only have added to his indignity: a fifty-eight-year-old man—yes, he remembered his age—reduced to the ultimate image of the juvenile refugee with a cardboard name placard draped around his neck. And added to his anxiety, too; it was difficult enough to keep the shirt on your back when it didn't contain your identity. Your name was supposed to be something no one could take away, and he had surrendered his.

CHAPTER TWENTY-FOUR

WHEN THE TRAIN STARTED MOVING, THE CLICK OF THE wheels came through the uninsulated floor slats with a quick, sharp rhythm that reminded him of his youthful departure from Krimsk. He had hitched a ride with the junkman Boruch Levi in his wagon, to Sufnitz. The Krimsker Rebbe had spoken harsh words to him, and he had found it ironic and appropriate that he should leave Krimsk accompanied by junk. At Sufnitz he had boarded the coach, and as they pulled away from the station, he sat in his long frock coat, hugging the box of books on his knees. He clutched it tightly, for he felt as if he were flying. The telegraph poles rushed to greet him and fled with equal alacrity to give others a chance to welcome and bless him. "*Mazel tov,*" they greeted him; "Welcome to the world." The click of the wheels, however, as the train sped toward Warsaw, convinced him that he had entered a new level of being. The modern world had its own twentieth-century language— precise, rhythmic, and metallic. Romantic that he was, he had imagined that all mechanical encounters had a lyric bent, enthusiastic and heraldic, like birds chirping at dawn.

And now forty years later in the cattle car, herded like a beast on the way to the slaughterhouse, he heard the modern language again through the bestial slats. Somehow, for all its certainty—so very precise—his death seemed a distant event. He had always lacked the more normal imagination. His hysterical mother possessed it, and she was right; this train was carrying her son to his death. He knew it, too, but it seemed strangely distant, veiled in the future. Even in the most peaceful years, he could never visualize his own personal life. Somehow he always seemed inchoate and incapable of further individual development, a partial person. Sometimes he had thought that he might have grown if he could have found a more complete environment. How could anyone learn to swim by just looking at the water? One had to go into it, immerse oneself in it. Since he felt incomplete, he couldn't marry; that would have been unfair to any woman. If he didn't know who he was, how could he ask anyone to share his fate? There were women, attractive and intelligent, who wanted him. They found him sensitive, intelligent, and unfailingly polite. They also found him caring, but in that they were wrong, or if not wrong, somewhat misled. He did want to care, but indeed, his limitations meant that he cared in a limited way, and he knew very well that caring was something that should not be subject to restraints.

He wondered about the world, he wondered about the Jews, and he wondered about himself in a most unrestrained manner, never drawing any hard conclusions but loving his speculative inquiries—always balanced. Since that intellectual balance wasn't life, he remained a marginal personality with many friends. Some of them wondered why he didn't marry, and others wondered why he didn't commit his prodigious talents to one of the causes that interested him. Ironically, his ability to visualize the future of an institution or a party made it impossible for him to join wholeheartedly in any such ventures.

When he left Krimsk, his mother had wept; his father, too, but still he had left, and he had rejoiced at the click of the train steaming along the tracks away from his boyhood home. Now, some wept and some didn't, but no one rejoiced.

CHAPTER TWENTY-FIVE

THE ROUTINE CLICK OF THE WHEELS ALONE, RISING through the open slats of the cattle car, would have been overwhelming, but one wheel wasn't working as it should. A thrashing, almost cannibal gnashing of steel devouring steel became deafening. It wasn't an even contest. How could it be? The maimed wheel, for all its turning, couldn't escape the track. The noise obliterated one's ability to think. Who could exist within such a pounding, beating roar? It was enough to make you forget who you were. In this he had an advantage over his fellow sufferers.

They left Warsaw accompanied by the crashing of the uneven, asymmetrical wheel. The more they traveled, the more lopsided the wheel became, until along with the terrible thumping din, their teeth rattled and their bones ached from the vibrations. Gathering speed, the train progressed into the countryside; all the while the physical abuse increased as the wheel degenerated—blow by blow, ceaselessly pounding. To him it seemed the purposeful extension of Nazi logic: there can be no limit either to Nazi vigilance or to the affliction of the devil-Jew. First you starve the Jew, then you imprison his dispirited body in an over-crowded railroad car, and finally, for good measure, you shackle the train itself with a flat wheel. Always the Nazis are thorough. Always the Nazis are teachers; let the Jews learn from the pitiless destruction of the chosen wheel. Fatigued, feverish, disintegrating, forced to turn, the wandering Jewish wheel perpetually encounters the fresh, cool, endlessly unrelenting Nazi track.

They prayed that it would stop, but it did not. Ceaseless, the insufferable pounding. His ribs ached; his head bounced off the swaying side of the tortured carriage. Ceaseless, the insufferable became sufferable. His ribs became numb. His head, a spherical appendage of the car, a harmless rattle in the noisy charge of the train into approaching darkness in the East. Behind him in the West, the shameless naked sun plunged below the horizon in a splash of brilliant bloodred rays. Inside the carriage they were shielded from only this natural obscenity and no other.

Ceaseless, ceaseless, and then the miracle occurred. The train stopped. At first the miracle went unrecognized. The memory of the din continued to echo in their ears, reverberating as loud as the original sound. The train sat still on a siding, but their bodies continued to suffer, experiencing real agony in a phantom journey.

As their senses returned, so, too, did their pain, and so, too, their voices. Moans filled the dark car as agony spoke, its voice surprisingly sweet, surprisingly gentle. A soft cloud of torture hovered above them in the tomblike car, tantalizing them with the forlorn illusion that their journey had ended. They had broken through and crossed a barrier of pain, but geographically Dzika and Stawki Streets with their spacious, light, airy holding yards could not be many kilometers behind. Although they had not entered the East, clearly they had left the West forever. As if to emphasize the irrevocability of their departure, the sun hurriedly buried itself beneath the horizon, leaving the still train in a thick vein of darkness.

In the woods alongside the track, crickets began their nervous, insistent, conversational twitter. At irregular intervals singular, deep-voiced bullfrogs hiccupped their soliloquies of rapture and appetite into the night. Birds' wings stirred the close, blind air, their chirps and trills telling of darting and sailing not far beneath the stars. Had any of these creatures, or even the stars themselves, stopped to listen to the alien carriage parked in their midst, they would have thought it a phantom train. Black, motionless, slumbering in the middle of nowhere, it emitted dull, cooing, dovelike moans, the effluvia of former lives. Pinioned in slow, dark pain to the rough boards, he would have agreed, imprisoned in his suffering body, his tortured flesh crushed in the vise of other bodies, all locked into the immuring cell of the cattle car. Motionless, the cars imprisoned between the insensible parallel prison rails. The entire train shrouded without by the cool night and permeated within by a warm miasma, so that it was impossible to lift even a finger.

Frozen in the confining matrix, his face sagging against the wooden slats, he felt that the cool night air only inches from his parched face was impossibly distant, incapable of providing him with breath. Phantoms cannot use fresh, cool air. Only the soft cloud of torture, inches above their heads, sustained them. Only that poisonous cloud was capable of motion and therefore of nurture. This moist creation drew from them, as if by evaporation, the shed and unshed tears of their own sorrow, the heat of their hearts, the soft soughing of their breath, their very life force. As they stood motionless, their lives ebbing away, the cloud seemed to condense sufficient traces of dewlike, life-giving nurture to sustain them. The exchange was poisonous, for they were all losing more than they received; nevertheless, it seemed to sustain them. They even valued it, as the only nurture they had. They found the poisonous vapors soft, sweet, alive, and life giving. And illusory as it was, they were right, for without it, they would have expired even more quickly.

A phantom cloud sustained phantoms. When he heard voices in the thick vapors behind him in the car, he knew that the miasmal cloud had provided the energy. It therefore came as no surprise that they were phantom voices, last season's uprooted corn shocks drifting against each other in a slight wind: dry, rattling, accidental echoes of lives once lived.

Exhausted, parched by thirst, he paid no attention to them. Disembodied phantoms could not be expected to alleviate thirst or hunger. Jewish phantoms could be expected to complain, and he didn't need disembodied spirits for that. He heard them talking in scratchy whispers, as if there could be no substantial voice without a body. As they spoke, they seemed to find their voices. What first attracted his interest was their tone. The phantoms seemed to be disputing some point or other. This wasn't at all like phantoms, and it drew him to their exchange. One voice was questioning. Had it had more energy, it would have been cross-examining, but it was exhausted. For all its desultory persistence—it paused before pursuing its line of inquiry —it seemed the voice of the inferior phantom. The socially superior answering voice acknowledged the right, even the duty, to question. Because of their mutual weariness and shared assumption of inquiry, their discourse seemed to fall somewhere between discussion and debate.

Although their disputatious tones had aroused his curiosity, he wasn't sure what was the topic of contention. From remarks about "giving the child bread," he realized that the Yom Kippur fast had ended. He also surmised that the superior voice wanted to give some of their food to a boy, whereas the inferior voice challenged this, since they lacked sufficient food themselves. He quickly understood that these were "rabbinic phantoms."

"He's just a child," the superior responded. "Just a child," the voice repeated with pity.

"What difference does that make?" the junior questioned. He seemed frustrated at the display of feeling for the child.

"So young," the senior voice sighed in melancholy regret, as if he had not heard the question.

"So?" his interrogator persisted. "Doesn't one's own life come first?"

"Yes, but we—shall not survive," the senior voice uttered wearily.

With his mouth pressed against one of the boards of the cattle car, he could not have joined the conversation had he wanted to. But he was offended by the lethargic resignation of the senior voice. Never mind that he himself had lost the will to live. Never mind that he had surrendered to despair some time ago; he was offended that rabbinic phantoms had done so, and especially the more senior rabbi. What kind of faith was that? What kind of leadership? In outrage, he seemed to be grinding the wooden beam into sawdust and choking on the fine, dry particles. The indigestible wood tasted so similar to the dessicated bread crumbs they were discussing! But that was the point, wasn't it? One was an obscene cattle car, and the other was—why, the other was the staff of life, and the senior rabbi didn't seem able to distinguish between them! Had the Nazis turned both of them into termites? He wanted to spit the wooden board out of his mouth, but the accumulated pressure of his fellow passengers seemed too great to overcome. So he bit down upon the wood like a vengeful termite and waited for the phantom to continue.

The first voice was that of the younger, junior phantom. "Then why didn't you permit her to switch the child?"

When no immediate response followed, the loyal termite feared that the senior phantom had simply faded away, drifting back into the sickly sweet poisonous cloud that hovered above them.

"She would have had to provide them with another child, and you know the law: one may not surrender one soul of Israel."

"Yes," the junior voice conceded. "That's the Mishnah, but in the Gomorrah's discussion aren't there mitigating circumstances?"

The senior voice didn't respond at once, and the junior pressed his argument. "Doesn't the Gomorrah quote a case in which a group of Jews are traveling along, and they meet a band of goyim who demand that they surrender one Jew to be killed, or if they refuse, then the goyim will kill them all? In that case, all must be killed. But if the goyim specify their victim, then one teacher says that only if the intended victim has rebelled against the legitimate kingship of David may his fellows surrender him to the goyim and certain death. The other teacher, Rabbi Yochanan, however, decrees that even if the selected victim is not guilty of any crime, they are still permitted to surrender him to their enemies; for if they don't, they will all be killed, including the one singled out, whereas if he is surrendered, then the others may live. In either case, the one singled out has only the most momentary life expectancy. So indeed if the goyim single out a victim, then his fellow Jews may surrender him. And hasn't Hitler singled us all out?"

The junior voice fell silent, awaiting the expected reply. The termite's anger dissipated, however, into careful consideration of what he had heard. Indeed, the termite casually chewed on his generous helping of wood with a certain dedication as he ruminated on the phantom's charge. Although he wasn't familiar with the particular talmudic citations, the termite had no trouble with their frame of reference; he knew that the Mishnah, the part of the Talmud that had been written earlier, was the basic codification of the oral law, and that the Gomorrah contained the later accumulated commentaries on the Mishnah. The debate sounded vaguely familiar, which came as no surprise, since he himself as a young man had once been part of the talmudic world. As for their discussion itself, the junior phantom's suggestion sounded quite plausible. In either event, the intended victim who had been singled out was as good as dead, so why shouldn't he be surrendered to the enemy? As for Hitler singling out every Jew, that, too, could not be disputed. And if it were, one could rely upon Rabbi Yochanan's position. By surrendering the one Jew, who would die in any eventuality, all the others could be saved. That certainly made sense. So why hadn't the senior rabbi permitted the children to be switched? How could anyone or any rabbi know where any child would be safer?

Hadn't he, the termite, once learned something or other like that? It seemed familiar, but different, too. The Talmud that he had learned—What was it? When was it?—had never seemed so reasonable. He was trying to recall, without much confidence. After all, what kind of memory did a termite need? If you can't chew it, you don't eat it. It must have been from his days as a young talmudist in Krimsk. Hadn't the Krimsker Rebbe called the termite a bug? vermin? And where else had he learned Talmud? While he was puzzling over these questions, the senior phantom began to speak.

"You do not remember all of the Gomorrah's discussion. Although in theory Rabbi Yochanan was correct, the law in this case is not decided on the basis of his logical inference. The Gomorrah relates an actual historical case. A Jewish fugitive fled to the city of Lod, where he sought refuge with Rabbi Yehoshua Ben-Levi. The governor's soldiers arrived in pursuit and surrounded the town. They announced that if the fugitive were not surrendered to them, then they would destroy the entire town and everyone in it. Rabbi Yehoshua Ben-Levi went to the fugitive and successfully convinced the man to surrender himself in order to save everyone else. The man agreed and surrendered himself to the soldiers for execution, and the entire town of Lod was saved.

"But the story doesn't end there. There are dreams, too. The prophet Elijah, may he be remembered for good, used to reveal himself to the great Rabbi Yehoshua Ben-Levi in his dreams. Suddenly the Prophet ceased to appear. The great rabbi fasted many fasts. At long last, the prophet Elijah reappeared. When Rabbi Yehoshua Ben-Levi asked him why he had disappeared, the prophet Elijah retorted, 'Shall I reveal myself to those who surrender souls?' The great rabbi strenuously defended himself: 'And didn't I act in accordance with the Mishnah that explicitly teaches that if the intended victim is singled out, he may be surrendered?' Elijah answered him, 'But is this the Mishnah of the pious?'"

There was quiet, and when the junior phantom spoke again, his voice was no longer challenging. Reflective and chastened, he asked, "And that is the halacha, the law?"

"Yes, that is how Moses Ben-Maimon decides the law, and after him, the *Shulchan Aruch*, the definitive code. No less than the great Genius of Vilna maintains that the lawmakers follow this Gomorrah in which the logical inference is overruled by the prophet Elijah's declaration in Rabbi Yehoshua Ben-Levi's dream. 'But is this the Mishnah of the pious?'"

There was silence in the carriage, almost as if out of respect for the nocturnal appearance of the prophet Elijah. The senior phantom added, "So even according to the Gomorrah, there are no mitigating circumstances; one may not surrender a soul of Israel."

"Let me give the child some of my bread first," the junior rabbi responded, and then he announced to the boy's mother, "Madame, I am giving your son some bread."

The mother did not answer, although the termite thought he heard the sounds of the starving child ravenously swallowing. He wasn't certain about that, because he was no longer paying careful attention to the voices. He was thinking about the Gomorrah's discussion of the Mishnah, and in particular about the prophet's appearance in the rabbi's dream, and he was marveling at the way visionary prophecy—or was it prophetic vision—had overruled the human intellect when it came to choosing between lives. Having lived in the ghetto, the termite knew what an awesome and horrifying task it had been for well-intentioned good men who had been forced to make such decisions. Alas, the prophet Elijah had not appeared in their dreams, but would it have helped, since all of them had been singled out by Hitler?

The termite, the wet, saliva-soaked wood still in his teeth, had to admit that the old-phantom-senior voice was not that of a termite. No, the prophet Elijah had revealed himself through the Talmud to the old rabbi, too. Certainly the prophet Elijah would not reveal himself to a termite or to a phantom. The Germans had tried to turn the Jews into termites and phantoms, but with some they could not succeed, because even though all had been singled out, some refused to surrender even one soul of Israel.

As the termite thought about that, the wood in his mouth began to taste foul. The termite of course in his wooden dreams had never seen Elijah, but as the discussion progressed, some of the terms seemed more and more familiar. Hadn't he heard it all before? But wasn't it different then? Where was it? When was it?

And suddenly he knew. Suddenly he remembered. Yes, it had been back in Krimsk, when he was substituting for his old primary instructor Reb Gedaliah and teaching the Mishnah to the young boys on the eve of the very fateful Tisha B'Av in Krimsk when the rebbe had returned to the world with such disastrous effects. So he did know about not surrendering a soul of Israel. He himself had taught it to those boys on one of his very last days in Krimsk. That night he had met the rebbe and confessed his doubts, and the interview had become so very bitter. The rebbe had called him a heretic who would never escape Krimsk because there was always enough space for vermin. But his doubts that the rebbe rejected were not based on the Gomorrah; hadn't his doubts somehow focused on the Mishnah? Weren't there two rabbis arguing about what you could do and couldn't do to save property? Something about preventive destruction. Yes, that was it, and he was teaching those young boys on the eve of Tisha B'Av about the *terumah,* the priestly tithe on produce in the days when the Temple still stood in Jerusalem. The Mishnah was discussing cases in which, to save something pure, one could purposely make it impure; now he remembered that, in the final case, everyone agreed that the Jewish women could not surrender one of their number even if the goyim threatened to "make them all impure." Yes, that was the Mishnah he had heard quoted at the beginning of the discussion about not surrendering one soul of Israel, and it was that Mishnah that had irritated him so in his youth, because there was no way of saving the Jews.

Now, having experienced the Nazis' hell and having heard the discussion of the Gomorrah, he wasn't so very irritated at all. On the contrary, having heard the developmental discussion, he found the Gomorrah's conclusion satisfying, intellectually and emotionally. That such a cerebral, analytic document as the Gomorrah should recognize that there are some cases that man cannot judge was delightfully surprising. Deciding the law by a prophet's chastising appearance in a rabbi's dream seemed esthetically pleasing. It was the warm, personal relationship with the heavenly that he had always assumed should be appropriate for a Jew with his God. If he no longer believed in God, he thought ironically, might he still believe in His prophets? He supposed so; he certainly accepted the Gomorrah's teaching that you could not believe in rabbis—or at least, that you could not rely on their intellect alone. He rather enjoyed the idea that such a supremely rabbinic— and caviling—document as the Gomorrah openly admitted the limits, even the failing, of the rabbinic intellect. That might not affect his beliefs, or the lack of them, but it must affect his attitudes. The older rabbi was certainly no phantom, and he certainly was no termite! The Gomorrah was very impressive indeed.

Suddenly it dawned on him that he had been teaching those boys only the Mishnaic tractate about the priestly tithe; there was no Gomorrah on the Mishnah! That particular order of the Mishnah, almost one-sixth of the entire Mishnaic compilation, was almost completely devoid of the Gomorrah, the later commentaries! The Gomorrah on it had either never been written down or had been lost. So what were those rabbis talking about? They couldn't have made it up! They weren't phantoms, were they? Feeling absolutely unlike a termite, he spat the wooden bar out of his mouth and, bracing both his hands on the board and his body against the carriage wall, he thrust with all his might, first arching his back against the bodies piled upon him, and then, when he had inched them back, pushing against the wooden bar with all his strength until his face barely cleared the wooden slats. To his surprise, the crushing weight behind him seemed to lessen, as if the bodies were made of earth and, once shifted, they simply collapsed with all their primordial dirt into that new position.

Although his face was only an inch from the wall, with all the impetuous passion of his distant youth he managed to shout, "But there is no Gomorrah!"

As soon as the words were out of his mouth, he regretted them. He received no response. He sensed that the rabbis stood in shocked silence. His pronouncement must have sounded as scandalous to them as if he had shouted, "There is no God!"

"No," he corrected himself, "I know there is a Gomorrah, but I don't understand"—this statement struck him as overwhelmingly sincere—"the Mishnah you quoted originally is in the tractate of Terumah, and that Mishnaic tractate has no Gomorrah at all."

Apparently he had atoned for his unintentional offense, for within moments the younger rabbi answered him.

"Yes, you are right," the rabbi began cordially, even respectfully. "The Babylonian Talmud has no Gomorrah on the tractate in question, but the Jerusalem Talmud does. That's the Gomorrah we were discussing, the Jerusalem Talmud."

"Oh, the Jerusalem Talmud," he said aloud in respect-ful amazement.

All his life he had admired knowledge, and tonight he had learned something, something very satisfying. He was particularly impressed that the rabbis knew the Jerusalem Talmud. Although both talmuds commented on the same Mishnah, the entire Orthodox Jewish world studied the Babylonian Talmud, which was codified later under less repressive circumstances and tended to be more complete, somewhat more relevant to life in the diaspora, and less elliptical. Indeed, the legal tradition had developed almost exclusively around the Babylonian Talmud. Anywhere in the Jewish world, if anyone heard the words *Talmud* or *Gomorrah,* he could safely assume that the Babylonian Talmud and the Babylonian Gomorrah were under discus-sion. Only the most accomplished rabbis were conversant with the Jerusalem Talmud. It came as no surprise that the younger rabbi was not so well versed in the Jerusalem Talmud. Indeed, it would have been a surprise if he were. It did explain the younger rabbi's reverence for the older man. That was not misplaced; the younger man was fortu-nate to have such a teacher. Well, he was, too, even if he had only overheard their discussion.

He was overwhelmed with amazement as well as re-spect. In his impetuous youth, he had assumed that he had known all there was to know. So the Jerusalem Talmud commented on the problem with a sensitivity and insight that he could now appreciate. He knew that forty years ago in Krimsk he would not have understood such a discus-sion. Ironically, the codified law was as stringent as he had thought it was. As a youngster, he probably would have focused on the severity, without appreciating how soft, almost sensual, the discussion was that led to that final decision. No, as a youngster he had been interested only in his own dreams, not in those of some ancient rabbis. Now he identified with old Rabbi Yehoshua Ben-Levi in the city of Lod, who had in all good faith mistakenly surrendered the victim to his tragic fate. It seemed an act he himself was capable of—in some ways something he had been doing to himself throughout his life. The ancient rabbi's dreams were also satisfying because he no longer had any of his own.

He began wondering whether the Krimsker Rebbe knew the Jerusalem Talmud. He probably did, since as a young man the rebbe was reputed to have been one of the more brilliant talmudists in Poland. His own father came to mind; his mother, too, amidst a wistful feeling of melancholy, but that was suddenly replaced by the sense of horror that a mother had faced earlier on this Yom Kippur day when she had asked the rabbis if she could surrender a soul in Israel for her son.

"May I ask you something? How did the mother accept your decision?" he asked tentatively, betraying his embarrassment at a curiosity that seemed almost prurient under the circumstances, but which he found irresistible.

Peremptorily, the senior rabbi answered in stern disapproval, "One doesn't discuss such matters in the presence of the parties concerned."

"Yes, of course, I'm so sorry," he stammered. He might have added, "I didn't know," but he was too busy thinking in startled awareness: I should have known. Rabbi Yehoshua Ben-Levi's dream was her own very personal nightmare: she was shrieking because she had accepted the awesome decree of the Jerusalem Talmud. Yes, it was *her* hysterical screaming that had drowned out the barking of the Nazi dogs. That mother had been shrieking because her son was here. Mother and child were both standing behind him in the car. Perhaps immediately next to him; no, the shrieking had not been that close. But not far away, either. Both silent and hungry. He felt ashamed that he had no crumbs to spare for the boy. Had he fasted on Yom Kippur, he might have. Although it was irrational, he felt bad that he had not fasted; he wanted the rabbis and the mother to know that if he had any crumbs, he would give them to the boy.

"I didn't fast on Yom Kippur, but I wish that I had. Should I begin fasting now?" he asked abruptly.

He certainly didn't believe in God; it thus was irrelevant for him to fast, but logic had failed, and perhaps there were more ancient rabbinic dreams that might lessen the darkness. He knew that he did not know enough, and he was determined to answer honestly any of the rabbis' questions.

"Who are you?" the younger rabbi asked curiously, with a hint of suspicion.

Expecting them to ask why he had not fasted on Yom Kippur, he was surprised by the very question that had frightened him earlier. Then he had been embarrassed, but now he was troubled; if he told them that he didn't know his name, it would lead them far afield from his question. On the other hand, if he described himself and omitted his name, it would disingenuously suggest that as a sinner he was too embarrassed to reveal his identity.

"A Jew who has forgotten his own name," he said honestly, but with some hesitation.

To his surprise, he received a direct reply from the older rabbi.

"First remember your name," he ordered.

"I can't."

"You must be strong," the old man urged.

"To survive this, we would need the strength of stones," he replied, using the phrase from the Bible.

"Yes, you do."

"I do?" the termite wondered.

"Yes, the midrash in discussing our trials teaches that if stones fall on a clay cooking pot, woe unto the pot: if the pot falls on stones, woe unto the pot. In any event, it is woe unto the pot. But the midrash continues and suggests that we are the stones, because in spite of all our sorrows, our holy nation will survive. Where is pharaoh? or Bilaam? or Balak? or Haman? Hitler, may his name be erased, he, too, will join them no matter what becomes of those here."

The train lurched and began moving again.

CHAPTER TWENTY-SIX

THE JOLT WITH WHICH THE TRAIN OVERCAME ITS inertia flung the mass of captive bodies back into their original traveling positions. In an impersonal act of physical abuse, his fellow travelers simply collapsed silently upon him, thrusting him forcefully into the wall once more. His head banged into the slats, but on the rebound he managed to catch the wooden reinforcing bar in his teeth. Still damp from his own saliva, the wood was softer than it had been on original encounter; he was prepared to hold it patiently in his veteran bite until the next stop. He hoped, of course, they would stop soon. His ribs ached, piercing pains laced his back. Terrible cramps seized his legs. His bruised head seemed to buzz with a dull soreness. Resigned and stoic as he was, the pain was real. He desperately wanted his and everyone else's torment to cease, but he had adjusted as well as he could to such slow torture.

But now he had another reason for wanting the train to stop, a positive one that he savored with a growing sense of excitement. When the train stopped, and they left the carriage—it no longer seemed like a cattle car, for it carried noble people in whose dreams the prophet Elijah appeared —then he would meet the rabbis, the mother, and her son. He would meet them, and see what they looked like. He would talk to them, and perhaps they would become friends. Perhaps he would serve the wise, older one as a disciple. Deep down, he understood that the older one would disapprove of him—and rightly so, for he had never gotten on very well with the Krimsker Rebbe or any other rabbinic authority figure. If the truth be told, he was quietly rebelling against the rabbi's authority at this very moment. Although he still didn't know his own name—was it really so important after all?—he was fasting. No longer a termite, he savored the cellular wooden bar in his teeth because it filled his ravenous mouth, making it impossible to eat the remaining scraps of bread, which he was determined to give to the boy.

The older rabbi would probably discern his rebellious ways at once. How could one fool a wise, suffering man like that? In spite of his contempt, the younger rabbi was likely to find him somewhat intriguing, and in spite of the senior's disapproval, the latter would have a serious inquiring relationship with him. It had happened before. For all their disapproval and lack of tolerance, such scholars were fascinated by outsiders and had a strange need for them, with their erring ways, to validate the scholars' orthodox view of the world. And if neither rabbi wanted his friendship, at least he could stand next to them. After all, they shared the same journey—and presumably the same fate, just as the Jews of Lod had. Yes, he could stand next to them when they prayed, sit next to them when they ate, and best of all, he could lie next to them when they dreamed. He could manage without their approval; their company would be enough, and of that he was assured, for they were fellow passengers on the train from Warsaw.

He felt differently about the mother and her son. He desperately wanted to be involved with them and to be liked by them. Right now he was fasting for the boy. As mad as it seemed, he had the strange presentiment that he was about to become a father. He would comfort, feed, protect the boy. The law decreed that one must not surrender one soul of Israel! Just as the boy's mother had accepted that decree, so, too, he would not surrender his love, nurture, concern, protection, for this child, his child, even until death. He had no intimation that the death that would terminate such paternal aspirations would be not his but that of the boy, and that it was only minutes away.

For the moment, in spite of the discomfort, he had a deep sense of satisfaction at participating in the great drama unfolding behind his back. He took pride in being one of the group of Jews traveling along who would not surrender one soul of Israel. He took comfort in the fact that his immediate fellow passengers were crushing him against the wall; might this not provide the boy with more space and more air? Might this not dissipate the poisonous cloud above his head? He even discovered hope, not so much for himself as for the boy. They were traveling to the East, toward Babylonia and toward Jerusalem. Yes, he was hopeful that he would even remember his name, but he was not stone; he himself could not imagine the strength of stones. In this he remained himself, a heretic, for he could not appreciate the wisdom of the rabbis.

He also failed to appreciate just how disastrously one of the carriage wheels was not cooperating in the journey, and how it was giving rise to a more noxious cloud below.

With paternal sacrifice and collegial hope, he suffered his face to be pressed so far into the cattle car slats that while he was biting the support bar, his nose was pushed practically outside the car. Ironically, this painful, sacrificial disjointment of his facial features saved his life.

CHAPTER TWENTY-SEVEN

THE IMPRISONED GROUP OF JEWS IN THE DAMAGED carriage jolted eastward in bone-crushing weariness. Somewhere in the East lay Babylonia and Jerusalem, but their track led only into the deeper shadow of Polish darkness. The uneven wheel produced a bumping, rising and falling effect, as if a cripple were trying to run—as unnatural and destructive as though through some mad suspension of nature's laws, a sailing ship could sail on land until it thrashed itself to pieces upon the firm, solid earth.

The gyrating of the wheel grew louder until it was their entire world. It was as if they had stuck their simple heads into the center of the earth, and the whole imperfect planet was spinning lopsidedly through their ears. As the train increased its speed, the wheel ceased to revolve altogether, locked into position like a crude metal runner. The pulsating vertical pounding immediately ceased and gave way to a mad horizontal swerving as the carriage careened along the track at forty miles an hour. Inside, the travelers were slammed from side to side with such force that it seemed they might be crushed by the battering walls before the carriage jumped the rails. This unexpected mayhem was accompanied by the metallic screech of the frozen wheel grinding against the never-ending track. Had they not been previously stunned by the earlier thrashing, the higher-decibel shearing stress of steel would have proved deafening. It felt as if the devil had reached into their brains to stimulate the greatest pain that sound alone could produce.

Anything that terminated the sound would have been a relief, including leaving the rails with only the flimsy frame of the cattle car for protection. The flange of the broken wheel, however, remained sufficiently intact to keep the car on the rails, and the intense friction increased until the inky darkness in the east was dispelled by a false dawn. A bouquet of sparks burst forth from the impossible encounter, and following the headlong dash of the train, they arched, cascading outward and upward in a luminous arc that, had it been on the distant horizon or in the sky, would have suggested astral origins and eternal voyages. For those immediately above, the flashing streaks of light meant the sharp, bitter sting of sparking metal in their nostrils.

On the opposite side of the car, he was far enough back in the carriage that the earsplitting screech lost its deafening intensity. With his nose between the slats, however, he suffered the sharp, choking bite of the ozone and reflexively began to draw his head inside. But there was no space, and he no longer had the strength to move anyone behind him.

The false dawn continued as spark after spark—thousands, myriads of them—dashed into the dry wooden floor. Initially the Jews sniffed the clean, warm, robust aroma of singed wood instead of the corrosive metal. This proved a momentary respite as the first bitter vapors rose from the floorboards and billowed into the carriage behind the damaged wheel. Slowly the acrid smoke gathered in the lowest areas like a cloud of mist. Thick, warm, and suffocating, it ascended in humble, silent splendor. The paralyzed wheel shrieked below in metallic agony. The Jews above strained to breathe the sweet, phantom vapors that had seemed to sustain them earlier and now represented their only hope. Unrelenting, the fiercely real, thick, dark, stifling smoke rose to envelop the phantom vapors. The passengers fought for breath in paroxysms of choking coughs that managed to expel the hideous poison that had replaced the fetid air. Once they had expelled the smoke, however, there remained no choice but to inhale more of it—thicker, warmer, and even more deadly.

His face buried in the latticed wall, he, too, gagged on the smoke behind him, but he was sustained by the onrush of cool, sweet air. Only when the train began to brake and the slipstream eased did he think that he might be overcome; but even then enough oxygen reached him that he felt the train slowing, at last stopping in a final, wrenching bump.

He could hear the hurried steps of hobnailed boots along the tracks, then anxious calls: "Here it is! This carriage! Water! Get water over here!"

So much activity surrounded the car that he didn't hear the water hissing on the smoldering boards. He did hear the orders directing the boots. "Under the carriage; the board there. That's it!" When the fire had apparently been extinguished, he heard the arrival of more booted troopers and the barking of guard dogs surrounding the car. Aroused by the smoke and the late-night excitement, the dogs snapped in as loud a chorus as had those back at Dzika and Stawki Streets. Yet he didn't think of the ghetto; that seemed so impossibly distant. He thought that finally they would have to open the damaged car.

The commander instructed his men to be alert and make certain that no one escaped, for they were responsible for "all the vermin," and they would have to deliver them all. As exhausted as he was, he felt a sense of thanksgiving at having survived.

After they pried open the door on the other side of the car, the commandant called, asking what the situation was. The inspecting soldier met a black cloud and gagged. "Smoke," he coughed. He was ordered to step back and let it clear. After what seemed like a very long time, the soldier stirred in the doorway. "They suffocated! Dead!" he called in revulsion at the vomit-stained corpses. "All of them?" his commandant inquired anxiously. "I don't know. I think so." This statement was greeted with curses and then the order to have the dead vermin thrown off the carriage and counted. This last order was accompanied by the urgent plea to unload and detach the damaged carriage and get the train moving again as soon as possible; it was already late, and they had to clear the line for other traffic.

Others clambered into the car and began prying the bodies loose one from the other and then tossing them down to the ground. He wanted to announce that he was alive, but he stood exhausted, listening over his shoulder to pulling, scraping, and the dull thuds of the falling bodies hitting the ground, all punctuated by the occasional grunts and heavy breathing of the slave laborers as they strained at their arduous task. On the wall near him they discovered someone alive and promptly reported it to the officer. "That would only complicate matters," the officer said, but he ordered the man to hand the live ones down carefully, since as a transfer point they had orders only to expedite whatever they received.

CHAPTER TWENTY-EIGHT

WHEN THE ASPHYXIATED BODIES BEHIND HIM WERE removed, he fell. Before he crumpled completely onto the floor, two bloody teeth landed at his feet. When he saw them, he put his hand to his mouth and felt the sticky ooze of his own blood. He realized that the crossbar had knocked his teeth out while the swerving car bashed about the tracks. As sore as he was, he felt no additional pain at the discovery. It was irrelevant.

As they reached for his legs to drag him from the car, he raised his hand to signify that he was alive. With no facial response whatsoever, the Jewish slaves simply released his feet, reached for his arms, and mechanically hoisted him to a standing position. They guided him across the car to another worker, who sat him down in the doorway. Saying, "Easy now," the man pushed him forward, and he stumbled out of the car and onto the ground.

The cool, fresh night air had a bracing effect, and to his surprise, he staggered without falling. A guard motioned him toward a railroad tie, where several other survivors sat huddled in exhaustion. Although none was bleeding, they were completely dazed, slumped over, staring vacantly at the ground. He dropped down, joining them on their low perch. He took several tentative breaths and, discovering that he could breathe the air, several deep ones. He quickly slowed down because of the soreness in his chest, but he had never known air to taste so light and sweet. In and out, he slowly continued to consume the precious treat. He purposely did so quietly so that his captors would take no notice of his enjoying their air.

Somewhat revived, he looked around. A powerful floodlamp bathed the open area around the damaged carriage in bright light. Behind him were several buildings, but they squatted quietly in the dark, surrounded by the ubiquitous barbed wire. Beyond the train he had been on, he could see lines of freight cars and a number of tracks. It seemed to be a transfer point along the main line. Apparently Warsaw trains stopped here only when there were problems. The military personnel in the transport unit certainly seemed to have had experience with previous Warsaw trains. The agitated commander, a middle-aged captain, hopped about as if he were standing over the hotbox in the smoldering car. Well, now it was his problem. Let him solve it.

When the final bodies were tossed out onto the ground, the two laborers jumped down from the carriage and were sent away under guard. He was surprised that the pile of corpses by the track did not increase, in spite of the plentiful number that had been flung from the car. Then he noticed why. A great quiet hulk of a Jew was picking them up with such lumbering ease that they appeared doll-like as he carried them away and stacked them in the shadows under a roofed area. The steady, diligent giant had been removing them as fast as the two in the carriage dropped them out of the car. Suddenly he wondered where "they" were. Since they had all been behind him, he knew they could not have survived the smoke. Only seven or eight hapless souls sat next to him on their makeshift bench; clean-shaven, not one appeared to be either of the rabbis. No, they were all dead. He stared at the dwindling pile of bodies to try to identify the boy's small frame, but all he could see were the bodies of adults.

The mother had been right; the boy would have been better off remaining behind in the ghetto. But he couldn't help believing that the rabbi had been right, too. Sometimes there was no choice. From their drama only he remained; they were only phantoms, if that. Only he and the prophet Elijah knew what had happened. He would have preferred more reliable witnesses. Shmuel Zigelboym was a reliable witness, but he couldn't testify as to what had happened on the train. Poor Zigelboym, he had enough testimony to give without this. Strong Zigelboym, blessed Comrade Artur, knew without the dream; he had refused to lift a hand to help the band of goyim. Perhaps Elijah was appearing in Zigelboym's dreams in London right now. He wondered whether Elijah would appear in the dreams of a Bundist; probably he could, but not in the same form that he did for Rabbi Yehoshua Ben-Levi in Lod. He had an inexplicable faith that the vision would be communicated.

A sharp, commanding voice interrupted his reverie.

"They must all drink. This is a transport unit, not a ghetto. We forward exactly what we receive, no more, no less. They come in alive; they go out alive. Those who arrived dead will present no problem. Neither will these," the officer commanded.

"Yes, Herr Captain," answered a dull voice.

The great large man had left his work with the dead for the time being and was working with the living. With a bucket and ladle, he was making his way down the line, doling out water. Some who sat were too stunned to drink. The man shook someone's shoulder not unkindly.

"You heard the captain. You must drink."

He put down the bucket and with one hand pried open the man's mouth while slowly spooning in the water. At first the recipient gagged, but then, surprisingly, he drained the entire ladle and then another two. The surplus liquid dribbled down his chin. Watching the man's animal reflex, he realized how thirsty he himself was and wished the hulking giant would hurry. As the bucket approached and his fellow passengers drank greedily, he had the panicky feeling that there wouldn't be any water left for him. His eyes were riveted on the bucket; it was all he could do to keep from pouncing upon it and swallowing it all.

When his turn finally arrived, he tore the ladle from the man's hand and uncontrollably swallowed it all in a single gulp. He pushed the ladle back to have it refilled and just as ravenously swilled the second. The man took back the metal spoon.

"I'll bring more," he said dully, turned, and shuffled sturdily away. At his side in his large hand the bucket looked ridiculously small and toylike. It also seemed very rigid and unbending; the large man's head seemed somewhat flaccid by comparison, lolling slightly to one side as if he were some unfinished sort of Nazi automaton. Waiting for the bucket's return, he wondered what they had done to make the giant that way. In spite of his dull looseness, he kept moving at a workmanlike pace that added to the impression that he was some kind of robot manqué.

In a few moments he reappeared, rounding the corner of one of the nearby buildings, water sloshing from the full pail. He stepped into the floodlit area and approached the group of survivors. The giant's face seemed to possess hardly any more tension than the water. Although his body contained great strength and even awkward lumbering grace, his face was slack and witless. His mouth hung open, accenting the lack of control. He was balding, light puffs of blond hair clustered about his head. Unshaven blond hairs covered his face, but these, too, poked out like limp strands of hay. The spotlight found no expression to highlight in his dull eyes. It seemed as if the Nazis had even appropriated the Jewish golem for their diabolical purposes. As the retarded giant neared him, there seemed something achingly familiar in that blond imperfection.

Rising slightly from the log in amazement, the thirsting man rasped aloud in confounded disbelief, "Itzik Dribble?!"

In their hometown of Krimsk, this retarded giant had been both the hapless butt of a generation of malicious children and an essential participant in the most inspiring spiritual moment the community had ever witnessed. Cruelty to such an unfortunate child came as no surprise to anyone but the constant victim; heroic spirituality—that was a surprise, and it had occurred almost forty years ago.

After five years of complete and unexplained absence from the life of his hasidic town, the Krimsker Rebbe had casually strolled into his beis midrash one day as if he had never been gone for more than a few minutes. The hasidim gazed in astonished silence. In response to the childish gossip about the squat Krimsker Rebbe's resemblance to a frog, Itzik had been led to believe that the rebbe *was* a frog. As the community stood in amazement, Itzik dashed forward and asked if it was true that the rebbe was a frog, and the Krimsker Rebbe calmly responded that indeed it was true. Poor Itzik then wanted to know if it was also true that the rebbe prayed by jumping like a frog. When the rebbe responded, How else would a frog pray? Itzik pleaded in expectant delight for the rebbe to show him.

To demonstrate, the saintly, reclusive Krimsker Rebbe took the dull-witted boy's hand, and together, before the entire congregation, they climbed onto the reading table and leaped together in prayer. Then the rebbe told the poor child an inspired tale of a wondrous magical frog who helped a slow-learning but well-meaning child become a great success and perfect son. All who saw such a thing treasured those moments forever. You could forget your name in the Nazi hell, but you could never forget such righteous beauty.

And he had just now called him "Itzik Dribble."

CHAPTER TWENTY-NINE

AS SOON AS THE WORDS HAD ESCAPED HIS LIPS, HE
regretted having used the derisive nickname from the alley-
ways of Krimsk. Itzik, however, was not at all offended,
which made it all the more shameful. At the sound of his
boyhood name, Itzik was so taken aback that he literally
stopped in his tracks. The bucket continued its momen-
tum, splashing almost half its contents before the handle in
Itzik's hand reined it in, but Itzik took no notice. His dull,
simple face had been seized by an expression of childish joy
usually reserved for red balloons or pony rides. Even then
something vacuous remained around his eyes and mouth,
for he was no child. The giant looked down at the man who
had addressed him. Not recognizing him, Itzik became
confused. A pained sadness reflecting years of abuse flashed
across his brow; if he didn't recognize the man, how could
he have heard his name? He slowly stepped forward.

"Hello, Itzik," he repeated very slowly and very warmly,
reassuring the poor soul that he did indeed know him and
that he had addressed him by his childhood nickname.

Heartened by the affectionate tone, Itzik approached him and leaned all the way over, practically touching his forehead to the top of the man's head as he unsuccessfully scrutinized him.

"Who are you?" Itzik asked quietly, fear flickering in his voice.

"I'm Yechiel Katzman from Krimsk," he answered without the slightest hesitation, pronouncing his own name before he was aware that he had remembered it.

Yechiel was surprised and fascinated, too, that his name had reappeared so spontaneously. Any real joy or sense of triumph, however, was outweighed by his concern for poor Itzik Dribble, who seemed so pathetic and painfully vulnerable. And, Yechiel had remembered his own name only because of Itzik. Without the pitiful Itzik, Yechiel would still be going around like a . . . like an idiot, he had thought earlier. It was poor Itzik who had saved him from that cruel, self-inflicted appellation.

"Shraga's brother?" Itzik asked, his voice rising emotionally.

"Yes. Our father Nachman Leib had a leather shop off the lane to the creek."

"You used to help Reb Gedaliah, the children's teacher?" Itzik blinked his eyes in triumphant recall.

"Yes, that's right. I used to substitute for Reb Gedaliah."

Overcome with excitement, Itzik opened his mouth and began to wheeze in hoarse, heavy breaths. Drool formed on his lowered bottom lip and dribbled down his chin. Yechiel reached forward and took Itzik's free hand, clasping it in both of his own. "It's all right, Itzik. It's all right. We're together."

A look of incomprehensible delight in his unfocused eyes, Itzik put down the bucket and took Yechiel's small hand in his large ones. Itzik began to rock back and forth, emitting a low moaning sound. Yechiel coaxed him to a halt by holding Itzik's hands steady and asking, "Itzik, how are you?"

Itzik stopped rocking but continued to moan.

"Sh-sh-sh," Yechiel quieted him. "Yes, we're both from Krimsk."

Itzik smiled weakly at the mention of their hometown. "What are you doing here?" he asked.

"I came on the train from Warsaw," Yechiel explained, as if it were the most common of journeys. "We had mechanical troubles and had to stop here. I suppose they'll be sending us on soon."

"No, don't go," Itzik said, his eyes large with fright.

Yechiel couldn't tell whether Itzik knew where the trains were going. The engine was backing the front of the train into the station; with a jolt that echoed through the cool night, it rejoined the carriages that had been behind the burned car.

"No, no!" Itzik cried in fright.

"I wish we could stay together," Yechiel said sadly, in complete sincerity.

Fear still in his eyes, Itzik said, "Come, come with me!"

CHAPTER THIRTY

Without waiting for Yechiel to respond, the powerful Itzik pulled Yechiel to his feet and started across the yard. "No time. Hurry."

When Yechiel stumbled, Itzik put his large hand under his elbow and, practically hoisting him off the ground, brought him to the remaining corpses by the track.

"Work! You must work!" Itzik said.

So saying, Itzik lifted a bearded corpse by the shoulders and motioned for Yechiel to take the feet. "Work!" he urged frantically.

Yechiel reached for the dead man's feet, but he barely had enough energy to lift his own. He stumbled to his knees.

"Itzik, I can't," he gasped.

The giant lifted Yechiel with one hand and the corpse with the other.

"Hold him like you're helping."

Itzik released Yechiel, and Yechiel obediently clung to the corpse for support. With Itzik carrying both the dead man and Yechiel alongside, they staggered toward the roofed area. Once in the shadows, Itzik carefully deposited the corpse on top of a sizable, neat pile and ordered Yechiel to hide behind the stack of bodies. From the temporary safety of the shadow of death, Yechiel watched Itzik return to his grisly task. As Itzik carefully placed a body on top of the pile, Yechiel examined his townsman's handiwork and found it impressive. Itzik had stacked the bodies crosswise like cordwood to the height of five prone corpses. Yechiel was surprised that Itzik's meager intellect was capable of such planning. He wondered whether it was a skill the Nazis had taught him through considerable repetition.

After the cool, refreshing night air on the other side of the enclosure, he was overwhelmed by the putrid smell of vomit from the corpses. In the terror of the cattle car he hadn't noticed. Now he realized that the vomiting must have been a reflex of asphyxiation. He couldn't help noticing that many had frozen in the most grotesque positions. Had he been overcome by smoke while squashed against the wall, his appearance would have been no less macabre. He ran his tongue across the wounded fissure in his gums where his teeth had fallen out, and it didn't even seem a disfigurement. Yechiel concentrated on watching Itzik go about his basic task, to and fro, to and fro.

Most of the bodies were buried under others, but he could distinguish many, and it seemed an embarrassment that they should lie so very degraded and exposed. He knew that they were dead, but it seemed cruel that they should be so debased. He didn't want to see the rabbis' bodies, although he had practically ridden to safety on a bearded corpse. He couldn't even hope that a particular body was not one of the rabbis; if it weren't, it was still someone else's, and he couldn't take pleasure in some other Jew's death; not one soul of Israel! He didn't want to see the mother's remains; but above all he didn't want to see the boy's small corpse. In fact, he was so fearful of seeing the child's body that he found himself drawn to the pile to make sure that it was not in his field of vision. God, how he wanted to mourn over the boy's body and ignore it all at the same time! He concentrated on Itzik's coming and going to avoid the shackles of death. After all, he thought ironically, didn't the Nazis say, "Work liberates"?

The next moment he witnessed a lesson in liberation. A portable wooden ramp was brought alongside one of the cattle cars. To the accompaniment of the guard dogs' barking, the door was pried open; the guards and dogs advanced several steps to make certain that no one tried to exit. Unlike the taut soldiers and straining dogs, Yechiel was not surprised that no one came dashing out of the overcrowded, sealed car. The captain had the survivors from the burned car marched from the railroad tie over to the ramp and ordered Itzik to load them into the already packed cattle car.

One by one, Itzik picked them up in a workmanlike way, lofted them above his head to a horizontal position, and tossed them into the car onto the heads of those packed vertically shoulder to shoulder. Yechiel was horrified at how Itzik picked the victims up, swung them into a prone position above his head, and with two hands casually flung them onto the shelf of heads as if he were merely loading bales of hay into a barn. What distressed him even more was that none of the straw men raised any objection. From his hiding place he couldn't hear whether anyone inside the car complained, but he guessed not. With all the live passengers save Yechiel back on board the train from Warsaw, Itzik closed the door, the guards sealed it, they all descended the ramp, Itzik pulled it back, and with a blast of its whistle, the train slowly moved out of the lit station into the darkness of the night. It resumed its journey as routinely as any train in the world, even though this train was born in darkness and was headed toward resettlement in the East.

Itzik returned to clearing the last few victims of the Warsaw train. When he finished, breathing heavily, he fell to the ground near Yechiel.

CHAPTER THIRTY-ONE

"Where's the train going?" Yechiel asked.

"Treblinka," Itzik answered.

"What do they say about Treblinka?"

"They say we're better off here."

"Why?" Yechiel inquired gently.

"It's not so bad here," Itzik explained.

Yechiel realized that Itzik knew less about Treblinka than he himself did. In the ghetto rumors had abounded; now he believed them.

"You look very good, Itzik," Yechiel said kindly.

"I have been blessed with great strength. Captain Pizer knows he can rely on me," Itzik said proudly.

"Captain Pizer?"

"He's the commandant. He works very hard to keep the railroad running, and I help him. It's very important. You know there's a war on?"

The question was not at all rhetorical, but asked in all seriousness.

"Yes, Itzik, I know."

"Good. Some people don't. They act like there is no war, and that gets Captain Pizer very angry. . . . But I know."

Yechiel nodded in acknowledgment.

"Captain Pizer will be happy that you're here. You can help him, too. You were one of the smartest people in Krimsk. I remember," Itzik said proudly.

Itzik reached over and put his hand on Yechiel's leg. Yechiel held it tenderly between his small hands. Then Itzik pulled his hand away and looked at Yechiel in fear.

"What is it, Itzik? What's wrong?" Yechiel continued to speak as gently as he could.

Itzik looked as if he wanted to say something but was afraid.

"Itzik, what is it? You can tell me. I knew you as a little boy in Krimsk. You don't have to be afraid."

Itzik seemed uncertain.

"Itzik, I am very happy that we found each other. It's not good to be afraid, and it's not good to be alone. Now we are together."

Yechiel reached over to stroke Itzik's hand. The dull giant welcomed his townsman's touch, but he frowned.

"Well, I'll probably be going soon," Yechiel apologized.

"No, don't go. Please don't go!" Itzik cried and squeezed Yechiel's hand.

Yechiel blanched in pain.

"I thought you didn't want me here."

"No, don't go! Please!"

"At least we're together now, Itzik."

"Were we friends in Krimsk? I don't remember," Itzik asked.

"I was several years older, and I don't think you were in

one of my classes, but we used to see each other. Sometimes you came to play outside the primary school and we talked. Yes, we were friends. Not best friends, but very respectful friends," Yechiel stated definitively. "And we are friends now. Special things like friendship last a very long time."

Itzik smiled.

"I remember," he said proudly, "that you used to stare outside the window when you were teaching, and behind you the children threw spitballs."

"You see, we were friends," Yechiel announced triumphantly.

"You were nice to me. You never teased me. All those boys in the school, they called me Itzik Dribble, but you never did, did you? . . . You never did until tonight."

Itzik delivered this not so much as a complaint as a description of things past and present.

"Yes, I'm sorry."

By way of apology he wanted to confide in Itzik that he had forgotten his own name, but knowing that would only confuse the poor soul, he said, "It won't happen again."

"Am I dribbling now?" Itzik asked in a petulant tone.

"No," Yechiel answered.

"You see!"

"Yes, I see. I'm sorry."

"Have I dribbled since you came here?" Itzik demanded.

"No, of course not," Yechiel lied. He regretted having added the "of course not." He was a poor liar. "Let's not talk about it, Itzik. There are so many nice things we can remember."

"Like what?" Itzik asked curiously.

"Close your eyes, Itzik. Go ahead," Yechiel encouraged.

"That's it. You're back in Krimsk. You can see it. You're looking at something that makes you happy. Tell me what it is."

With his eyes tightly closed, Itzik groped in the air in
front of him as if they were playing blindman's bluff.

"I'm running along with Uncle Barasch in the field
near the factory, and we're catching yellow butterflies."

"Are the butterflies very pretty?"

"Oh! They're beautiful. So beautiful that when we
bring them back to the house, they make Mother cry. But
they don't make Uncle Barasch and me cry. We laugh when
we catch them."

"That sounds wonderful. You see, there are so many
good things to remember."

They sat quietly for several moments.

"Yechiel?" Itzik asked.

"Yes?"

"Can I open my eyes now?"

"Yes, of course."

"Do you want a turn?" Itzik asked. "To remember," he
explained.

"All right. I would like that," Yechiel agreed.

"Close your eyes, Yechiel. Go ahead. That's it. You're
back in Krimsk. You can see it. You're watching something
that makes you happy. Tell me what it is, Yechiel!" Itzik
begged in excitement.

With his eyes tightly shut, Yechiel saw his family sitting
at the supper table. He had just come home from the study
hall, and his father, brother, and sister were already eating. A
kerosene lamp lit the room. It seemed to be autumn. He
wasn't wearing a heavy coat, but it was already dark. His
family seemed so sweet, so hardworking, so loving, so inno-

[2 3 0]

cent. Feeling as if he were about to cry, he closed his eyes even more tightly. His little sister seemed so close that he could reach out and touch her soft brown hair. Was that why Itzik had groped blindly with his hands? Had he been picking his way through a host of golden butterflies? Poor Itzik.

"Tell me, what is it? Go ahead, tell me, Yechiel?" Itzik implored.

"I'm in the Krimsker Rebbe's beis midrash, and the rebbe wants to pray with a pure soul because the rebbe doesn't want to pray alone. He chooses a very, very good boy and he prays with him in a very special way that only rebbes know how to do. They jump like—" Here he hesitated. Had he gone too far? But no, Itzik was clamoring, "Frogs, frogs!" in great delight. "Yes, they jump like holy frogs. And all the Jews in the beis midrash are happy to see such a perfect prayer. And the little boy's father is very proud that the rebbe chose his son to pray."

Yechiel opened his eyes to see Itzik sitting with his eyes and mouth wide open in glee. Spittle dripped down his chin. Yechiel overcame an impulse to dry it with his sleeve. Itzik began to moan softly, and the spittle only increased. Yechiel saw it falling onto Itzik's pants leg, but mercifully, he couldn't hear it.

As Itzik sat dribbling, Yechiel pictured the young boy leaping on the table with the rebbe, praying like a frog, and he remembered the rebbe's prediction that night: Yechiel would never succeed in leaving Krimsk. Hadn't the rebbe said that he would walk in Warsaw? Well, as a journalist, he had done plenty of that! The rebbe had also said that Krimsk was just the right size for him. And that was correct, too. He could never flourish anywhere as he had in

Krimsk. He had always held himself back from fully joining into political life because of his skepticism; he never
married because he didn't feel like a complete personality.

He hadn't gotten very far, had he? To Yechiel's playful
mind, Itzik Dribble seemed his twin: crippled by mind,
alone, unable to marry, and in pain. Clever as the comparison was—for it contained the cleverest of ironic truths—
he regretted it, embarrassed by the self-serving pathos he
was so easily given to. He, Yechiel, was fully responsible for
what he had or had not become. Itzik was not. No, Yechiel
was not Itzik's brother. To suggest that was unfair to Itzik.
Yechiel might console, might encourage, might even make
Itzik happy, but to do so he would have to take responsi-
bility for his townsman. Itzik needed him not as a brother
but as a father, someone whom Itzik knew, who would
value Itzik's life above his own, who would never betray
him. Could Yechiel make such a commitment?

"It's my turn now!" Itzik implored.

"Yes," Yechiel answered, not quite understanding what
it was his turn to do.

Itzik, however, closed his eyes. "They're closed real
tight. I'm ready," he announced.

"What do you see that makes you very happy, Itzik?"
Yechiel asked softly.

"We are all sitting at the Sabbath table Friday night. It
is winter outside, cold and snowy, but inside it is warm
and full of light. Father and mother are at the ends of the
table, and I am sitting next to Uncle Barasch. Across from
us is baby Moshe. He is in his high chair eating noodles,
and we are all laughing at him, he is so cute. Mother is

happy. Later, Uncle Barasch will tell me a story and kiss me goodnight."

"Yes, that sounds wonderful," Yechiel agreed, but he felt an ache of memory that threatened to be debilitating. They weren't really in Krimsk, no matter how much they pretended.

"It's your turn," Itzik invited.

"Itzik, can you stay here?" Yechiel asked.

"It's not so bad here. Captain Pizer—"

"No," Yechiel interrupted, "can you stay out here with me tonight? Aren't you supposed to be somewhere?"

"They like me to guard the bodies. Captain Pizer says that I am the only man he can trust. The others take things from them, and then they trade with the soldiers. Captain Pizer doesn't like that. It's wrong. The soldiers are wrong, too. It's stealing. Even after they die, all things still belong to the Reich." Itzik delivered his words with great sincerity.

"What will they do with them?" Yechiel asked, aware that they sat protected by the shadow of death.

"Oh, I don't know that," Itzik said cheerfully.

"What will happen to them tomorrow? Will they stay here?"

"Oh, no. This is a transportation battalion. We'll put them on a train as soon as possible."

"To Treblinka?" Yechiel asked.

"For this many bodies we might get an empty car, but you never know. There's a war on. Did you know there's a war on? Did you know there's a war on?" Itzik asked very seriously once again.

"Yes, I did know," Yechiel answered.

"Good. Captain Pizer says we must never forget. I remember," Itzik said proudly. "There's a war on," he repeated, as if some message from his simple brain was continuing to revolve on neural circuits after it should have ceased.

"There certainly is," Yechiel agreed.

Yechiel yawned in spite of the war. No, he yawned because of the war.

"Are you tired?" Itzik asked.

"Yes, I have had a difficult journey," Yechiel explained wearily, as if they were not sitting amid a field stacked with corpses.

"Oh," said Itzik, not really comprehending.

"Can I sleep here?" Yechiel asked.

"Yes. Why not?"

In response, Yechiel shrugged and gingerly lowered himself from a seated position to lie on his side. He was very sore; his chest, back, and shoulders had tightened up in the cool night, and he groaned trying to find the least uncomfortable position. He rolled onto his back, but that proved no better. His eyes closed reflexively from the pain. When they opened, he saw Itzik staring at him with the same frightened expression he had worn when Krimsk was first mentioned. Yechiel looked directly into Itzik's worried eyes.

"Yes?" he invited.

"They said all those things."

"Who said?" Yechiel asked.

"Everybody. People shouldn't talk to you, they said. I remember."

"What did they say, Itzik?" Yechiel inquired.

"The rebbe threw you out of Krimsk, and that you were a—"

Not capable of remembering, Itzik came to a halt. He simply sat with his mouth open and his face frozen, as if someone had pulled out the plug on a machine. Apparently, Itzik's circuits were so poor that he was simply waiting for the message to arrive.

"A heretic?" Yechiel suggested.

"Yes, a heretic. That's a very bad thing," Itzik intoned. "I remember."

Overcoming the pain, Yechiel managed to sit up so that he could answer the grave accusations with more dignity.

"No, Itzik, they were wrong. It is not true. The rebbe told me—no, the rebbe promised me—that I wouldn't leave Krimsk even if I tried. He said that in some way I would always be in Krimsk. And he was right. Tonight with you I am in Krimsk."

Itzik seemed slightly relieved that Yechiel had not been thrown out of Krimsk, but he was still concerned. There was the other matter of that difficult word, so difficult to remember.

"You're not a . . . heretic?"

"Itzik, sometimes people think they know much more than they do know, and that gets them into trouble. Then when they find out what they don't know, they understand things better," Yechiel explained, but he had a hopeless feeling that Itzik didn't understand at all and that he, Yechiel, was not capable of presenting his thoughts in sufficiently simple terms.

"No, Itzik, I am not a heretic," he stated, and at that moment it didn't seem to be such a serious lie; he was determined that he was going to serve Itzik as a faithful surrogate parent.

"Promise?" Itzik insisted.

"Promise," Yechiel affirmed.

The fear disappeared. A promise was obviously sacred and inviolate.

"People say strange things. They like to gossip about someone if he is somewhat different. They can tell terrible tales and hurt a person badly. People live on foolishness. They can be very cruel," Yechiel said sadly.

By Itzik's nod of agreement, Yechiel saw that he did understand.

"You know what they said about me?" Itzik said indignantly.

Yechiel knew that it would be foolish, cruel, and hurtful to Itzik, but he also knew that Itzik's new father must know so that he could comfort the child and try to educate him to be less vulnerable.

"What did they say?" he asked apprehensively.

"They said Zloty or some other cat was my father," Itzik cried.

"That's very foolish and impossible. I hope you didn't pay any attention to them," Yechiel said, but from the pained outcry, he knew how useless his advice would be.

"That's what my mother said, but they did bad things. They said that Zloty and the cats fathered Freda the Fool from Krimichak, too!"

"They sound silly. Silly talk from silly people," Yechiel insisted.

"They said that if Freda the Fool and I would get married, our baby would be just like Zloty the cat!"

Itzik announced this with such horror that Yechiel suspected he believed it.

"Nonsense! Who were these people who said such nasty things? Such stupid things," Yechiel demanded.

"All the men from Krimichak. I couldn't leave town without them trying to catch me."

"Catch you?" Yechiel asked in innocent surprise.

"At first they tricked me. They told me that Casmir's cow had given birth to a three-headed calf. When I went to see, there was no calf, just Freda the Fool without any clothes. They locked us in all night. It was terrible. Freda bawled more than a three-headed calf, and she made pee-pee all night. I could have vomited from the awful smell. The constable finally found us and let us out. Father paid him to look for me."

"You were a very good boy," Yechiel began, but Itzik interrupted him.

"That made them mad. They wanted to show that they were right, so they kept after me. Coming from the mill, they trapped me on the bridge with pitchforks, but I grabbed one and beat the others. I broke their heads and ran home. Mother and Father were afraid they would kill me, so they sent me to a family in the old Jewish section of Lublin until it would be safe to return. But those goyim never forget. It never was safe, and I never returned."

Itzik uttered the last words forlornly.

"A Jew hits a goy in the head, and that's that. He'd better leave town," Itzik said as if he were quoting someone.

"So you were in the Lublin ghetto and then came here?" Yechiel asked.

Itzik didn't respond; he was still dwelling on the injustice of his exile from Krimsk.

"I tried not to hurt them, but I didn't know my own

strength. Captain Pizer says that I am the best worker he has."

"I am very proud of you. You have acted like a mensch, a gentleman, and a very brave Jew," Yechiel said, embracing Itzik and kissing the top of his head.

"When the war is over, they'll let us go back, won't they?" Itzik asked.

"I hope so."

"Not to Lublin, to Krimsk," Itzik said.

Yechiel had heard in the Warsaw ghetto what had happened to the Jews of Krimsk. They were summarily marched outside the town, shot, and flung into ditches.

"Weren't they nice in Lublin?" Yechiel asked.

"Very nice, but it wasn't home."

"But you saw your family, didn't you?"

"They visited me when they could. We went on picnics," Itzik said.

"That sounds very nice."

"No yellow ones, though," Itzik added by way of complaint.

"What?"

"No yellow butterflies in Lublin. I like them best," Itzik explained. "*They* couldn't visit."

"I understand: no yellow butterflies."

Itzik nodded, and Yechiel did understand. He crawled over to the blond golem and had him lie down, comforting him by gently stroking his powerful back and patting his head as one would a child's.

"Let me hear you say your prayers," Yechiel suggested.

Itzik closed his eyes and covered his head with his

sleeve. "Hear, O Israel, the Lord our God, the Lord is One," he said. He opened his eyes when he was finished.

Yechiel leaned over and kissed him on his broad forehead. "You're a very good boy. I'm proud of you," he said, aware that he was repeating himself. Then he, too, lay down.

"I love you," Itzik said in a small, weak voice.

"Yes, my child, I love you, too," Yechiel said and fell asleep exhausted.

CHAPTER THIRTY-TWO

WHEN YECHIEL AWOKE, A FEW MINUTES PAST SUNRISE, his first sensation was of the bone-chilling cool of the night and the damp clamminess of his body on the ground. The haze of the early morning swirled low on the horizon, and with the green filter of the forest, a pinkish glow arose in the east as soft streams of gray-white light swept toward them, gently and clearly illuminating all. As he awakened further, he felt something stiff against his leg. He started to sit up and discovered the neat pile of corpses. Still frozen in their spasms of asphyxiation, they greeted the dawn with bulging eyes and twisted limbs, softened by the beads of dew that hung on them like the patina of a very cold sweat.

He rolled over and discovered Itzik's leg knocking against him. Agitated, Itzik was staring at the station platform. Yechiel sat up and looked past the pile of bodies to see a steam locomotive, large driving wheels grinding slowly, bronze bell wagging and clanging in insistent greeting, and large billowing puffs of steam rising into the fresh sky. The lower part of the clouds rolled in the soft gray-white of the shaded morning, but the ever-expanding billows rose above the trees, caught the pinkish rays of dawn, and drifted purple and pink in the breeze like great circus balloons. The small black engine, huffing, puffing, and ringing its bell beneath the rainbowlike clouds, seemed a large child's toy. Behind the cheerful machine rolled the cattle cars, sealed and stolid as coffins. Through the engine's merriment, Yechiel could hear the inexorable metallic hum of small wheels on the track, punctuated by the clicks of the uneven rails.

The sound chilled his heart more than the damp dawn or the dew-covered corpses. Not only Yechiel was afraid. A frenzy of fear in his obtuse eyes, Itzik turned to him in terror. His voice squeaked in childlike fright.

"Yechiel, don't go. Don't ever leave me!" he implored.

The train slowed, the engine hissed, the bell rang louder, and Yechiel silently kissed Itzik's hand with the full flush of a father's loving lips. He felt the tightening fear of Itzik's hand. His eyes narrowed, his voice grew weaker; loving lips had kissed him good-bye before.

"Take me with you," Itzik begged in a whisper. "Love—" he croaked.

The train had stopped moving.

Itzik tilted his head to rest his cheek on Yechiel's small hand. The bell had stopped ringing, and the release of the locomotive's steam vented in infernal hisses. For a moment Itzik lay quiet on Yechiel's lap. The soldiers were already calling Itzik's name. Yechiel saw the anxiety in the dull giant's profile and felt the blind terror surge through the slack, loose face, freezing it in half-baked fear. Without thinking, Yechiel leaned over and embraced his suffering child, delivering a kiss that sealed his fate.

"Promise?" Itzik whispered, his eyes blinking stupidly in hope.

The train to Treblinka stood still in the dawn.

"Promise?"

Yechiel knew there was no other way they could remain together; the law of the transport was that whoever came in on the train had to leave on the train. And if the Krimsker Rebbe had told him that he, Yechiel, the heretic who doubted the rabbis, would never leave Krimsk because there was always enough room for vermin, he had also commanded him, "Do not underestimate evil." In his innocence, Itzik was willingly using his great strength to aid the Nazis. Yechiel did not have the older rabbi's faith that the Jews had the strength of stones, but Yechiel knew that he could not refuse his newfound son. He had heard the Jewish mother's cry; no true parent possesses a heart of stone.

"I promise!" Yechiel answered.

"You do?" Itzik asked fearfully.

"Yes, we have the strength of stones," the new father declared; that was what Jewish children must believe.

"Captain Pizer says that—" Itzik began, but Yechiel cut him off gently. "Sh-h-h-h! We are stronger."

CHAPTER THIRTY-THREE

INSIDE, THE TRAIN NO LONGER SEEMED A TOY TO Yechiel, but it didn't seem as real as it should have. The loading, the sealing of the door, the crowding, the discomfort of surging forward, all were real, but somehow these acts seemed distanced from his sentient self; they possessed a dreamlike quality in which everything appeared to happen as in real life but flowed smoothly in the most paradoxical manner. Each action was slower, but the entire sequence faster than in real life. He both participated and observed, flowing along with a wondrous fatalism and calm.

Yechiel imagined that was what Zigelboym must have experienced as he left Warsaw, crossed Europe, and arrived in London. Poor Zigelboym, he had done what was correct, but in doing so, he had violated his Jewish worker's soul. Not one soul of Israel! Yechiel was not Zigelboym's brother; he had not earned that privilege. Rabbi Yehoshua Ben-Levi and the prophet Elijah were Comrade Artur's brothers. And the rabbis and the mother who lay dead in the carriage behind them. The dead child lay in that car, too; the son Yechiel had never had. The mother had the courage Yechiel had lacked. Was her son's kiss less sweet to her than Itzik's was to him? No, it must have been even sweeter, and yet she was willing to separate to save her child. When the law decreed that she could not surrender one soul of Israel, shrieking in horror she obeyed. He died at her side.

Poor Itzik, taunted that Zloty or some other cat was his father, rejoiced to discover that his true father was not a cat but a termite. Yechiel the termite. But Yechiel felt at peace with being a termite. In a world filled with evil, there seemed worse fates. With the observer-participant dream-like sensations, the ultimate irony didn't amuse him. After a lifetime of indecisively avoiding commitments, he had made the most fundamental and gravest decision imaginable when he was certain that he was doing the wrong thing. After a lifetime of too many choices, he had no choice. He had been so decisive only once before, when he had left Krimsk; and now this second decision had returned him irrevocably to the very same Krimsk.

But these ironies didn't interest Yechiel. He was more interested in what he might say to Rabbi Yehoshua Ben-Levi and the prophet Elijah. He might say that Itzik was unwittingly helping the Nazis, or he might say that Itzik was doomed, but even if true, there was a difference be-tween the railroad camp and Treblinka. Yechiel knew the truth—not one soul of Israel—and where was there a sweeter, more innocent soul than his Itzik! No, Yechiel's defense, if he had any, was not intellectual. Let the prophet Elijah look into his son Itzik's innocent, suffering face—

"Promise? Promise?"—and say no. Maybe others could. Yechiel could not.

Only dreams gave Yechiel hope. Rabbi Yehoshua Ben-Levi had made a mistake, but he had fasted and continued to dream. Hadn't Rabbi Yehoshua Ben-Levi made his mistake because of his love for the Jews of Lod? And hadn't the prophet Elijah still appeared to him? So, too, Yechiel had been unable to accept the law of the pious. If he didn't live to see the prophet Elijah in his dreams, might he not be visited and instructed by Rabbi Yehoshua Ben-Levi? Not one soul of Israel!

An impatient, fidgety Itzik asked when they would arrive. A calm Yechiel kissed him and promised, "Soon, very soon." Tormented by discomfort and boredom, Itzik asked what he could do. Yechiel answered, "Dream, my son, dream. We are a people of dreams. We must never surrender our ability to dream. Dreams are our hope."

CHAPTER THIRTY-FOUR

THEY ARRIVED AT TREBLINKA. FOR FEAR OF BEING separated, Yechiel firmly clasped Itzik's hand as the carriage door opened. It was good that he had done so, for they were greeted by screaming storm troopers, whips in hand, cursing vituperatively as their vicious dogs barked. With their tormentors in pursuit, alongside and in front of them, the Jews ran from the cattle cars and were forced to undress. Those who moved too slowly felt the slicing burn of the whips, the bludgeoning of clubs, or the tearing canine tooth.

Seeing the fear in Itzik's blinking eyes, a naked Yechiel Katzman shouted above the bestial din, "I'm here, son. I'm here."

When they were forced to run again and Yechiel stumbled, only the first lash fell upon his bare back, for his son interposed his great body to protect him and unflinchingly absorbed the horrors. Nude and bleeding, Yechiel arose in pained dignity, for he knew who he was; not only a name but also a father in Israel.

And the children of Israel honor the parents who love them so. Chased naked the final exhausting yards, the old father stumbles, and the child whose hand he is holding sweeps him into young powerful arms and gently carries him forward. When the heavy metal door to the gas chamber slams shut, they stand together, hand in hand among the crush of bodies. The diesels start, and the gas begins to enter, acrid and harsh. The father sees the questioning terror in his young son's eyes, and the father says to him, "You must pray."

Holding the father's hand, the son begins the perfect prayer, leaping up and down like a holy frog as he had in his youth on the rebbe's table. The boy golem doesn't know his own strength and carries his neighbors with him, up and down. One more like this and the building would burst, but alas, there is no other Samson.

As Itzik begins to pray, Yechiel understands the source of the Krimsker Rebbe's anger and forgives him. Unlike Yechiel and Itzik, the rebbe wasn't privileged to die with the Jews, the souls of Israel.

The gas performs its lethal work, and Yechiel begins to fall, but he cannot, and he wonders, Is this the strength of stones? For the last sensation he has is of being pulled upward by Itzik Dribble toward—the dreams of Rabbi Yehoshua Ben-Levi, yellow butterflies, and—heaven.

SOUND WAVES

YECHIEL KATZMAN WAS WRONG ABOUT SHMUEL
Mordechai Zigelboym. In his escape from the Warsaw
ghetto and during his stay in London, Comrade Artur never
experienced anything in a dreamlike way. Zigelboym's
escape across Europe was perilously real. In London he had
hoped to find help for the threatened Jews of Poland, but
instead his life there was an unremitting nightmare: no one
cared about the destruction of the Jews of Poland.

By May 1943, only a small remnant of Poland's Jews survived, and they, too, were faced with annihilation. And no
one cared about them either. In a last desperate attempt to
awaken the "Polish government in exile, the Polish nation,
the allied governments, and the conscience of the world" into
doing something to save the remaining Jews, Zigelboym
committed suicide in protest against the world's indifference.

Perhaps time might have slowed down in that final
instant when Zigelboym pulled the trigger. When the bullet
raced through its mercilessly short trajectory into the side
of his head—in that thousandth or a millionth of a sec-

ond—he might have felt as if he were dreaming, but even then Zigelboym would have been reminded of the few thousands of Polish Jews who still remained and the three million who had already perished—and it would only have extended the nightmare.

Although Yechiel Katzman was wrong about Zigelboym, he was right about the Krimsker Rebbe. It was precisely this point, the sharing of the people's fate, that so inflamed his reaction to Zigelboym's protest suicide. In addition to his accusing the Polish government in exile and the Allies of an apathy that bordered on the criminal, Zigelboym had written in his final note, "I can no longer remain when the surviving remnant of the Jewish nation in Poland, whom I represent, continues to be exterminated. My fellows in the Warsaw ghetto fell with weapons in hand in a final heroic struggle. I was not privileged to die as they did, together with them. However, I am one of them, and I belong in their mass grave. . . . I know what little value human life has these days, but since I was unable to effect anything with my life, perhaps by my death I shall be able to pierce the wall of apathy of those who have the means at this very late hour to rescue the few who remain alive. . . . My life belongs to the Jewish nation in Poland, and I, therefore, bequeath it to them."

When after the war the rebbe learned of Zigelboym's letter, he became positively frantic. He despised the godless Bundist for the criminal act of taking his own life. He considered making the long journey to London in order to spit on the apostate's grave. He cursed Comrade Artur for having surrendered to despair and having aided the Haman Hitler by doing his dastardly work for him. ("It is absolutely forbidden to surrender one soul of Israel!" So much more so, one's own!)

Initially, Zigelboym's suicide seemed the ultimate obscenity of an indescribably obscene era. But Yechiel had guessed right. The rebbe felt that he himself had deserted the nation, and should have shared its fate. Perhaps the rebbe could have sustained his anger against himself, but he could not sustain it against Zigelboym. After all, however foolish and however futile, Zigelboym was trying to save other lives. The Krimsker Rebbe came to realize that such foolishness could be born only of madness. In the suicide letter the rebbe found definite proof that Shmuel Mordechai Zigelboym had been mentally ill and not responsible for his murderous act. In the midst of the holocaust—after the futile revolt in the Warsaw ghetto—he had addressed his appeal to, indeed he had staked his life on, "the conscience of the world." In May 1943, only a madman could have believed in such a thing! If Zigelboym had physically escaped Treblinka, his wife and children and his poor, shattered mind had not. The Krimsker Rebbe came to recognize Zigelboym as one more victim of the Nazis.

The rebbe spent the war years in St. Louis in seclusion. Later, when the war ended and the rebbetzin learned that the people of Krimsk (or Kromsk, as it was called by its Polish masters) and almost all of European Jewry had been murdered, she feared that the rebbe would retreat from the world forever. To her astonishment, however, she was wrong. With energies that she didn't think he possessed, the rebbe emerged from his study and took the lead in organizing communal remembrances—through prayer, programs, and memorials—of the victims of the Nazi holocaust. When the rebbetzin expressed her surprise at his activities, he explained, "The world has no conscience. The question is whether *we* have a memory."

"They, the goyim, must remember, too," she said.

The rebbe shook his head. "They have no conscience, so memory is irrelevant. If we have a memory, then we might retain our conscience."

And the rebbe organized and attended meetings all over town. Effective leader that he was, his performance was flawed. Whenever another speaker mentioned "the six million," the Krimsker Rebbe was sure to interrupt, calling out, "And one!" When the speaker and audience quizzically turned to him, he would inevitably explain, "Six million and *one*. We must not forget Shmuel Mordechai Zigelboym, may he rest in peace." When a prominent university professor patiently pointed out that these were "round numbers," the Krimsker Rebbe informed him, "Some numbers you don't round off. Six million and one."

Because of his intemperate interruptions, the rebbe was no longer invited to participate from the podium at these community events. Ironically, the role of the "representative of a world that is no more" fell to Rabbi Max, the former bootlegger. With the demise of Prohibition, Rabbi Max became the official mourner of East European Jewry, precisely because, unlike in his disastrous bootlegging days, Rabbi Max no longer gave full measure; now he did permit the numbers to be rounded off to an even six million.

None other than Sammy Rudman had engineered the switch of rabbis. Although he felt it was an absolute necessity to replace the rebbe in order to effect the rebbe's own program, he felt as if he had betrayed him. In choosing Rabbi

Max as the replacement, Sammy had betrayed his father, too, who had never forgiven Rabbi Max and after twenty-six years still refused to speak to him. Sammy, however, who had served in General Patton's Third Army and seen at first hand the fate of his fellow Jews, insisted that they be remembered by someone who did know exactly what had been lost, and that Rabbi Max did know that. Moreover, Rabbi Max took it upon himself to say kaddish for the victims. That is, for the round number of victims. The Krimsker Rebbe himself said kaddish for Zigelboym. Indeed, he did it with such passion that Sammy suspected that even had Reb Zelig still been alive, the rebbe would not have assigned him the memorial task the way he had delegated kaddish for Tsar Nicholas II and Matti Sternweiss.

Sammy wanted to apologize for having replaced the rebbe with Rabbi Max, but he didn't know how. When his wife suggested a party honoring the rebbe, Sammy reluctantly agreed; he wanted to do something—anything!—for the rebbe, in whose home he had done much of his growing up. What would they all do at such a party? he wondered.

Sammy accepted his mother-in-law's offer of her lovely rose garden and began planning for a spring tea party in the rebbe's honor. The only problem, a very significant one, was that, as Sammy told his wife Bernadette-Brina-Bunny, he didn't think the rebbe would consent to such a celebration. Propelled by guilt and desperation, he went to seek the rebbe's permission.

As so often since his first visit as a boy, Sammy was received by the rebbe and rebbetzin in the kitchen. Feeling foolish, he broached the idea of a garden tea party in the rebbe's honor. The rebbetzin's strangely bemused expression did not help his confidence. The rebbe merely nodded and said, "I don't see why not."

Both Sammy and the rebbetzin looked at each other in disbelief to be certain that they had heard correctly. Indeed, they had. They stared at the rebbe, who smiled politely.

"Since it is to be my party, may I be so bold as to suggest the entertainment?"

"Of course, rebbe, of course," Sammy stammered.

"A string quartet would be acceptable, but if possible, what I would really prefer is a solo violin playing something very sweet and very romantic."

Sammy consulted with his mother-in-law, Grandma Polly, and his wife, Bunny. To have only one violin in the garden—a sweet, romantic one at that—seemed a little too kitsch, too shmaltzy. At their urging the rebbe agreed to have a chamber group play Vivaldi with a concluding violin solo, Bach's Chaconne in D minor from the Second Partita.

In the pleasant, sunny weather, the colorful, aromatic rose garden overflowed with guests, and the party went very well, far beyond Sammy's highest expectations. His wife and mother-in-law were particularly pleased that at the rebbe's request they had introduced Orthodox Judaism to Bach in their garden. They were hardly offended when the rebbe rose from his seat after the applause for the violinist had died down, thanked the musicians, then suggested that since there was a tradition of a memorial tea party in this very rose garden, this tradition should be continued. "We are, if nothing else, a traditional people," he declared. After the rebbe's kaddish for Zigelboym, the guests turned to sherbet and petits fours.

The kaddish for Zigelboym hardly dampened the festive

spirit, but a curious exchange occurred at the end of the party when the rebbe and rebbetzin were leaving, and it was even more mystifying.

"It was a lovely party, and I am most appreciative, but I must tell you, the violin that I hear is better," the rebbe informed his hosts.

The rebbe nodded and walked through the garden gate, leaving Grandma Polly, Bunny, and Sammy to turn to the rebbetzin for an explanation; but all the rebbetzin could provide was a smile of much appreciation and slight embarrassment. She didn't hear the violin. Only the rebbe did, and he said that it was very sweet indeed and very romantic. Since the early spring of 1948 he had heard it often, mainly at night and always from the East—the Middle East.

ALLEN HOFFMAN, award-winning author of the novels *Small Worlds* and *Big League Dreams,* and of the collection *Kagan's Superfecta and Other Stories,* was born in St. Louis and received his B.A. in American History from Harvard University. He studied the Talmud in yeshivas in New York and Jerusalem, and has taught in New York City schools. He and his wife and four children now live in Jerusalem. He teaches English literature and creative writing at Bar-Ilan University.